"Max," she said desperately, "there's something we need to talk about."

"No, there isn't."

He kissed her into silence, but she fought him off...tried to fight him off. He kept turning it into a caress or an excuse to deliciously imprison her arms.

"We must."

"We must make love first."

"But—"

"My darling...my darling..."

A hot, urgent kiss punctuated each seductive, caressing phrase.

"Oh, Max." Paula's strength failed her completely and she felt tears prick behind her eyes.

Lilian Darcy is Australian, but has strong ties to the U.S.A. through her American husband. They have four growing children, and currently live in Canberra, Australia. Lilian has written over forty romance novels, and still has more story ideas crowding into her head than she knows what to do with. Her work has appeared on the Waldenbooks romance bestseller list, and two of her plays have been nominated for major Australian writing awards. "I'll keep writing as long as people keep reading my books," she says. "It's all I've ever wanted to do, and I love it."

TOMORROW'S CHILD

Lilian Darcy

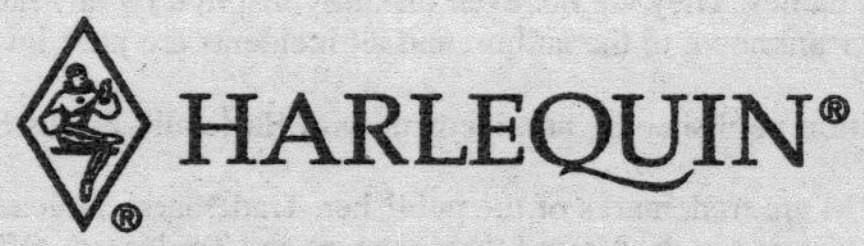

TORONTO • NEW YORK • LONDON
AMSTERDAM • PARIS • SYDNEY • HAMBURG
STOCKHOLM • ATHENS • TOKYO • MILAN • MADRID
PRAGUE • WARSAW • BUDAPEST • AUCKLAND

HARLEQUIN BOOKS
225 Duncan Mill Road, Don Mills,
Ontario, Canada M3B 3K9

ISBN 0-373-63191-X

TOMORROW'S CHILD

First North American Publication 2001

This edition published by arrangement with Harlequin Books S.A.

Visit us at www.eHarlequin.com

Printed in U.S.A.

CHAPTER ONE

PAULA knew that she had made the right decision almost immediately. In fact, she started to wonder why she hadn't done it years ago, but when she looked back and considered her life—all thirty-six years of it—up to this point, she realised that she couldn't have made the move earlier. There hadn't been time. There had been too much else to think about and to deal with. Now, though…

Arizona.

Moving quietly through her new courtyard garden at six on a March Monday morning, dressed in cotton chino pants and a loose blouse, Paula felt her spirits lift into the dry desert air. It was going to be another hot day. In the high eighties at least…

Although I'm going to have to stop thinking of that as hot, she realised. Because no one else in Zuma does. They wait until it hits at least ninety-five before bothering to use the word! It's magnificent, though. These cool, crisp, chilly mornings, and then the bake of the sun as it climbs in the sky, but the shade somehow always stays cool. Not like in the Midwest.

She had lived with Ohio's winter snows and summer steaminess all her life, and had never grown reconciled to them. This climate, she already knew, she would love.

The orange trees in her spacious courtyard were in flower, and their perfume was deliciously sweet, filling the air with fragrance. She had the well-concealed pump of her little fountain going so that the cool splash of water could be heard, and now, as she watered the newly planted earthenware pots of herbs she'd put in several days ago by the door, she heard the papery trill of a hummingbird's wings.

It was a sound that had startled her at first, a week and a half ago. The birds were so tiny and their wing-beats so fast and high-pitched that they sounded like some kind of large and nasty stinging insect. Her first instinct had been to beat them away with her hands, but then she'd got a good look and realised what they were—birds no bigger than the top joint of her thumb, with iridescent feathers and long, delicate black beaks.

She had stood very still that first day in the courtyard, as she was doing now, and after a patient, breathless moment one of the birds had alighted on her shoulder for several seconds, as if it knew that it was bestowing a gift. Since then she had always made sure to stop and watch. Now, still holding her breath, she saw the little blue-green jewel pause and cling to the leg of her dusty pink trousers, before flitting away again, out of sight, on to other business.

It was a timely reminder to Paula that she needed to do the same. She was starting work this morning at Catalina Canyon Pediatrics, as the newest partner in a practice of five pediatric specialists, and she knew that appointments were already booked for her from eight-thirty onwards.

As with most areas of medicine, starting in a new practice generally meant jumping straight in at the deep end, which meant that breakfast was a decidedly good idea—half a pink grapefruit, a single cup of decaf coffee and a large bowl of her own mix of wholegrain cereals and dried fruits. It was second nature to Paula now to be careful about what she ate.

She still had time for a shower, and then she dressed in the outfit she'd decided on last night—a confidence-builder and a good first impression, she hoped, with its silky texture, flowing lines and cool contrast of cinnamon and white.

A final assessment in the long mirror in her attractive desert-toned bedroom brought its usual mixed bag of responses. Her light brown wavy hair was nicely yet naturally styled and full of bounce, her brown eyes and finely drawn lips were lightly made up in silvery brown and cinnamon-toned pink, she hadn't left anything unfastened or untucked...

And no one who looked at her slim and softly curved figure in its smart blouse and full skirt would ever guess...

The usual twinge of pain and fear came and was sensibly put in its place.

Life was good! She had this beautiful adobe house with its oasis of a courtyard and its desert garden. She had work which she was sure to love here in Arizona as much as she had always loved it in Ohio. And she fully intended to take up at least two extremely relaxing and stimulating hobbies, which she would pursue with a degree of frivolity and dilettantism that would ensure that they never caused her the slightest amount of stress.

Pottery and saxophone, perhaps. Or calligraphy and parachuting. Well, no, on second thoughts, perhaps not parachuting. Maybe she would volunteer at the Zuma desert zoo... Yes, life was definitely good!

Even the way this move to Arizona had finally happened was proof of that. Paula's father and stepmother had retired to Florida several months earlier, thereby severing her only truly important emotional ties to Ohio, just as she was deciding whether or not to celebrate two very different anniversaries in her life—ones that didn't come equipped with any established traditions of cake and candles or gifts and champagne.

And then she had by pure chance run into her former chief resident in pediatrics, Brian Javitz, at a conference in Texas in January. They had ended up talking for quite a while, and when she'd found out that Brian and his fellow senior partner, Dr Max Costain, were looking for a fifth pediatrician in their Arizona practice things had just fallen into place...

She hadn't met any of the other partners yet. Apparently Brian's support and her own impeccable résumé of career milestones had carried enough weight. There had been an interview of sorts by conference telephone—more of a pleasant chat than a formal question and answer session—and then Brian had called back later that same day to state confidently, 'We want you. By March, if you can, because Wanda...Dr Hunt—she was asking you about your interest in allergies, if you remember...will be starting her maternity leave around then and we'll badly need the extra cover. Can you do it?'

Two months. 'I have to sell my house, wind things up with my current practice...'

'I bet they'll be sorry to lose you.'

'I'll tell them it's nothing personal. It's the climate, not the colleagues. And, yes, I'll be there in March, Brian. I'm looking forward to it very much.'

So here she was. She'd flown out for two days in early February, made a whirlwind tour of the city with a helpful realtor and quickly fallen in love with this house. She had finalised its purchase via fax and phone from Ohio, and had had all her things shipped two weeks ago, to coincide with her own arrival here after three days of hard driving.

She had enjoyed the journey, watching the landscape change as her comfortably luxurious car ate up the miles. Settling in had been a solitary pleasure—perhaps a belated and very private celebration of those November anniversaries she had ended up letting slide by. Brian had had her to dinner with his wife and teenage children last week.

'And you could come in for lunch and meet the other partners—Max and Wanda and Deborah,' he had said. 'Or—'

Paula had seized on the escape clause contained in that 'or'. 'Let's wait until I've officially started,' she'd said easily. 'We'll arrange something then. If Dr Hunt has a baby due any day, you're probably all pressed for time.'

This morning Brian was to meet her at the practice's office suite in the Catalina Canyon Professional Building at seven-thirty to show her over the place and help her unpack her things. The latter would consist just of books at this stage. She planned to decorate her new office with some whimsical personal touches, but needed to see it first.

Suddenly, she was intensely eager to get back to work. Despite several long walks around Zuma's parks, and sundry chats with various tradespeople and storekeepers as she'd set up her new house, Paula knew she had spent too much of the past week and a half alone, and that degree of solitude was not good for her.

Accordingly, and because she was not yet familiar with the drive, she set out at ten past seven and arrived ten minutes early, which then led to the slightly disconcerting discovery that Suite 220, Catalina Canyon Pediatric Associates, was still locked and unattended and she didn't have a key.

She frowned. Brian had said he would already be here.

She put down the box of books she'd carried up the external stairs and looked back along the railed balcony she had just walked the length of. It was still deserted. It overlooked a very pleasant courtyard, planted with a riot of desert colour and spiky greenery, and so she hung over the rail and looked at all this instead of merely waiting, and heard a woodpecker drumming a hole in the saguaro cactus.

Then she heard male footsteps echoing smartly on the tiled walkway below. Brian? Probably. She craned to look, realising at the same time that his route was the right way to come in future—through the shade and beauty of the courtyard and up this second stairway to her left, rather than taking the first stairway that faced the parking lot and led only past the other office suites on this upper level.

She couldn't see who was coming yet as he was almost directly below her now, but in a few seconds—if it *was* Brian—he'd be on the stairs and would turn at the landing to see her. She remained leaning over the rail, waiting for him, and felt the first rays of the sun clear the tiled roof behind her and strike the back of her head with considerable warmth, although it was still so early.

It wasn't Brian. She saw this at once as he attained the stairs. Brian was thinning on top and more than a little grey. He was cheerfully rueful about the former fact and rather pleased about the seasoning effect of the latter. This man, though, was neither grey nor thinning, but possessed a nicely full head of syrup-gold hair that glowed with rich highlights as the sun reached him as well.

He had a bunch of keys dangling from one hand and a mobile phone in the other, and when he looked up at her and held his key-laden hand across to jut from his forehead she realised that the strong sun behind her was making it impossible for him to really see her, despite the silver-lensed sunglasses that disguised his eyes.

She moved back into the shade just as he reached the top of the stairs, then stepped towards him.

'I guess Brian got held up at the hospital?' she hazarded. 'You must be Dr Costain.'

'Max,' he suggested at once. 'That is, if you're Dr Nichols.'

He smiled, which revealed even white teeth and creased his tanned cheeks. What the expression did to his eyes, though, she couldn't tell, because those silvered sunglasses were still firmly in place.

'Last time I looked.' She smiled back at him. 'But, if it's Max, make it Paula.'

'Paula.' He said her name slowly, as if tasting it, and she thought that she'd never realised it could sound so nice.

It was a name she'd always taken for granted. The female version of Paul. On Max Costain's lips, though, her name sounded like chocolate, rich and liquid and sweet, and a scant second after he'd said it he took off his sunglasses so that at last she could see his eyes.

Grey eyes, long-lashed, intelligent, searching, warm...and something else. It was there in his expression like the brief flash of a camera—and like a camera flash—coming unexpectedly, it seemed to blind and confuse her momentarily. Then it departed as if it had never been, leaving her exactly as she had been before...only somehow that wasn't quite true. Something was different but she didn't know what, and it flustered her.

'Let me unlock,' he was saying quite matter-of-factly as he reached for the door. 'Then I'll help you with that box. And you're right, by the way. Brian did get held up at the hospital. Problem with a newborn whose siblings already come to this practice. He should be here soon. In the meantime, forgive the lack of a formal welcome.'

'Formal welcome?' she laughed. 'I'm still waiting for *that* from my internship. What I got was more along the lines of, "Are you new? Here, put up this IV, take blood from Bed 4 and do a full gastric work-up on Beds 6 and 18."'

'Guess you must have trained in a pretty quiet hospital, then,' he said seriously, turning keys in two different locks, 'compared to me.'

It took her about three and a half seconds to realise he was joking—just long enough for her startled silence to earn his quizzical glance and crooked grin.

She responded with an upside-down smile of her own,

and drawled lightly, 'In that case, why don't I just concede defeat in the National Medical One-upmanship Stakes here and now and save us both a lot of trouble?'

'What, and deprive us of the pleasure as well?' he challenged plaintively.

She laughed, and he must have appreciated the open, silvery sound because he looked at her again, sidelong, his grey eyes glinting beneath a positive tangle of black lashes. Once more she shrank from the brief scent of danger—in anyone's book, he was an attractive man—and then, once more, she doubted the whole thing because his next words were so completely businesslike.

'Let me take that box and show you your office,' he said. 'Is there more to come?'

'Just two more boxes.'

'Why don't you give me your car keys and I'll bring them up while you unpack this lot?'

'Thanks.'

She made no attempt to argue. Heavy lifting with her left arm was something she needed to avoid whenever possible, and she knew she'd flouted that caution too much over the course of settling into her new house. So far she didn't seem to have done any damage. There was no swelling. But to have Max Costain offer like this, in a casual, practical way, meant that she could protect her arm without causing comment, curiosity...or understanding.

Hefting the box of books easily, he led the way through a waiting room decorated in grey, peach and sage green to a corridor from which several offices and examining rooms opened. Hers was the fourth office, looking onto the car park not the courtyard. It was rather small, and he apologised immediately.

'Rather than evacuating Wanda, who's only off for eleven weeks...'

'Has she delivered yet?'

'No, much to her annoyance. She's three days late,

and would much rather use her precious leave for *after* the baby's born. We're in the process of taking over Suite 222 next door, hence the mess and workmen you'll notice at the end of the corridor. Then this will become another examining room and you'll get a much cushier layout in the new bit.'

'So I shouldn't start buying prints and potted plants to match this decor?'

'Not yet, no. Be vocal in lobbying with Brian and myself for your preferred colours in the new suite instead. Now, your car...'

'Dark blue, right in front of the far stairs,' she told him, handing him the keys. The parking lot was empty enough at this hour to give him little trouble in locating it. In fact, he was probably parked in the adjacent space.

He disappeared, swinging her keys from one finger.

Too late, she realised she should have told him that she'd broken the key to the trunk of the car. He'd have to use the trunk lid release knob on the dashboard to get at those boxes. Well, he'd work that out for himself...

She turned to the pale wooden bookshelf that was built into one wall of her new professional home and slid her books into place—dense medical reference tomes, most of them, such as the Merck *Manual of Diagnosis and Therapy,* but also some volumes on allergies in children, which was one of her special areas of interest.

A couple of the books she used most went straight into the top drawer of her desk, and just as she shut it Max Costain reappeared in the doorway, carrying both the remaining boxes at once. They reached as high as his chin, and made the muscles of his arms bulge perceptibly beneath his blue shirt, but he was tall and broad enough to be able to manage them gracefully.

She could only be envious of his strength, and perhaps this showed in her face because he drawled deeply in an exaggerated Western accent, 'Now, where do y'all want the grand pianner, ma'am?'

'In between the potted palms, perhaps? Or directly under the chandelier?' she returned, while thinking desperately, He's *not* flirting with me. You couldn't call it that at all. It's just friendly and welcoming. He's trying to put me at my ease, which is nice because we're going to be colleagues. So I shouldn't mind it. But I do. I want to tell him to stop it, except that would make a big deal out of it and it *isn't* a big deal, and he'd think I was crazy. Or weird.

He was speaking again. 'Do you want to get the rest of them put away? Or would you rather have more of a tour? Deborah has hospital rounds this morning. She'll be in by eight-fifteen, I should think, and the office and nursing staff start at eight. The phone gets switched through from the answering service at eight-thirty but, of course, our private lines are open all the time.'

He had loped out of her office and was crossing to an alcove on the opposite side of the corridor as he spoke. 'Here's where we can make tea and coffee, though there'll be a better kitchen once we finish extending the suite. Brian and I tend to feel that the partners should get away from the practice for lunch whenever possible to clear our heads. Now, along here is where—'

'I guess I'm having the tour,' she drawled lightly, having followed him out of her office in order to keep up with the flow of words.

He stopped in his tracks, looked back at her and laughed. 'I guess you are. Sorry.'

'No, it's what I was going to choose, anyway. The books can wait.'

'Something else I should tell you first off, while I think of it,' he added.

'Yes?'

'I've roped you in for some new patients, without asking your permission first.'

'All my patients will be new, surely?' She frowned, a little suspicious of his grin of anticipation. Just what was he setting her up for here?

'These four will be very new, as we're hoping they won't be born for a few more weeks. Zuma's first set of quads.'

'Quads!'

'I've been asked to be their pediatrician, but I pointed out to the parents that they may want a back-up. They suggested a woman, and Wanda won't be back on board by then. Deborah has a lot on her plate, as she handles any of our kids with intellectual disabilities, so she was happy for me to offer the job to you. That is, if you want it...'

'Want it? I'd love to be involved with quads! We'd be there at the birth?'

'Yes, along with a hefty contingent of neonatologists from the hospital. The mother, Lisa Carey, is on hospital bedrest, of course, and they're hoping to keep the pregnancy going as long as possible. So far so good, but she's only just over thirty weeks. I'll introduce her to you when we're up there for rounds.'

They ended up talking for the next half-hour as they looked over the facilities and discussed the office routine, at which point Brian arrived, closely followed by office manager, Susan Clifford, and a clutch of women who filled various nursing and administrative roles and whose names and duties were far too much for Paula to keep straight all at once. She was content to realise that name badges would assist her at first, as well as her general familiarity with the routine of a pediatric practice.

With American medicine broken up very largely into specialty areas, a pediatrician in a private group practice filled what would, in many countries, be the role of a GP—only dealing exclusively with children, of course. Paula gave well-baby and well-child care, dealt with normal childhood illnesses and performed minor, office-based surgical procedures.

Also she was the first line of defence when it came to more serious problems and, like a GP, had to resist the problem of becoming lulled by daily routine. It was up to her to pick up as early as possible the often subtle signals of, for example, childhood leukemia or developmental delay, refer the patient on to the appropriate specialists and then integrate her knowledge of the cancer or the disability into that patient's general care. Good liaison with other specialists was therefore, a very necessary skill.

Apart from infected cactus spine puncture wounds and western diamondback rattlesnake bites—and she rather hoped that it would only be the hospital's emergency department that would encounter the latter—she expected that the work here wouldn't be very different from what she had known in Ohio.

And it wasn't. As always, she loved the pride and nervousness of first-time mothers, bringing their newborns in for a first office visit at two weeks of age. She loved the healthy wriggling of happy six-month-olds beneath her careful hands as she ran through well-baby check-ups. She loved the profligate distribution of their smiles and the splay-fingered batting of their little hands. She loved the funny little questions and comments from three-year-olds and the proud bravery of five-year-olds who 'didn't even *cry*.'

She loved the scientific minds of older children—'When you squirt the water in my ear, is it washing my brain?' She even loved the embarrassed relief of adolescents who were in the process of deciding that they were *far* too old to be seeing a children's doctor, but were very happy to have their more socially undesirable ailments dealt with, nonetheless.

There were only two more serious problems that came

to her attention during the course of the day. One of them was medical, the other was not.

The medical problem concerned a particularly moody teenager, Sam Hasher, aged fourteen, hitherto one of Dr Hunt's patients, who was brought in by his mother because his epilepsy, which had been well controlled until fairly recently with the use of a single commonly prescribed anticonvulsant, now seemed to be getting more difficult to deal with.

'I guess you'll have to put him on something else,' Mrs Hasher suggested to Paula hopefully. 'Can you give me a prescription that I can get filled today?'

'Well, it's not quite as simple as that,' Paula had to say. 'Let's try and work out if there's anything new that could be triggering the seizures first.' She ran through some questions about his diet, fitness and general health but nothing clicked so finally she asked casually, 'Sam, can you think of anything?'

He shrugged and said nothing, leaving Paula to wonder in silence, What is this? Teenage rebellion against his illness? Or something he doesn't want to say in front of his mother?

'Go on, Sam! Can you?' Mrs Hasher prompted impatiently. 'Speak to the doctor, don't just slump in your chair like that!'

'I can't,' he finally answered. 'There isn't anything new. Nothing's changed.'

He shifted uncomfortably, and that last phrase of his seemed to be giving him trouble.

Melanie Hasher was still impatient. '*I* can't think of anything. He's just growing fast. Could it be that? We don't have a lot of time today, Doctor,' she said. 'We've come straight from school. My daughter is in the waiting room, and we have to get home and get out again before... Well, we just have a busy schedule, that's all.'

Was this all it was? Paula was by no means sure, but

on her first day she wasn't going to tread on Wanda Hunt's toes by probing too deeply.

'We could try a second drug in combination,' she suggested slowly, watching both of them with a slight smile that disguised the depth of her scrutiny. Mrs Hasher looked relieved. Sam had narrowed his eyes, as if calculating something, and was still scowling.

'How do you feel about that, Sam?' Paula appended.

''S all right.' He shrugged, his expression closed.

'OK, then that's what we'll do,' Paula said briskly, and reached for her prescription pad. 'Now, it takes three or four days to reach full effectiveness, and I'm sure you're familiar with the way we start you at the minimum dose for your age and weight and increase it gradually to the point where it controls the seizures...'

Again she watched for a response, and again Mrs Hasher's impatient, harried look departed briefly to be replaced by relief.

'You mean you'll keep bringing me in here to check me and up the dose?' Sam said in weary disgust.

'Only if this first dose I've put you on doesn't control the seizures,' Paula said.

'OK.' He nodded, and there was now an air of defeat in his awkward adolescent frame.

Does he not want the seizures to stop? Paula wondered suddenly. What possible reason could there be for that? Is he getting some kind of emotional payback for his seizures? Attention? Special treatment? Tolerance for poor grades at school?

Convinced that there was a lot going on below the surface, she said only, 'I'll see you back again in a week, Sam. And there's no need for you to be here, Mrs Hasher, if you have errands to run at the same time.'

'Mmm, yes, I might.' The other woman nodded, already on her feet and reaching for the prescription. 'Now, come on, Sam, can't you?'

He muttered something under his breath, though he rose obediently.

Paula had several more patients to see after the Hashers had gone but they were routine, and when the last of them departed just after five it was Sam Hasher who drew her thoughts and had her sitting at her desk with her chin dropped thoughtfully into her hands for several minutes.

I'm going to spend longer with him next week, she finally decided. Especially if Mrs Hasher responds to that hint of mine and doesn't come in. There's an awful lot he didn't say today...

Home. It beckoned invitingly after the full day. She lifted her hair from her neck to let the cool of the air-conditioning freshen her, then stretched a little. Gathering her bag, she found Max Costain and Deborah Weir in conversation by the tea and coffee alcove, exchanging information about a patient both were concerned with.

The practice was quiet now, although two more patients still waited for Brian who had been a little behind all day.

'Off home?' Max asked her, breaking off from a technical description to Deborah.

'If there's nothing else...' She looked questioning.

'No, you're fine.' He shook his head. 'Go. I think we're all winding up, except Deborah who's on call and has a couple of hospital patients to see.'

Not wanting to distract them, Paula said a brief goodbye and left, reviewing her impressions of her new colleagues as she went down the stairs and through the courtyard, which was just gaining the shade from the opposite side of the building.

Deborah seemed nice. Short, cheerful, a little chunky. Brian she had liked and respected greatly during her residency, and he had an air of confidence and experience now which patients and their parents must respond to.

Wanda she had yet to meet. The nursing and support staff seemed pleasant and efficient.

And Max Costain? Somehow she wasn't as eager to reach a conclusion about him…except that those silvered sunglasses he'd been wearing this morning must have intimidated her to an unreasonable degree because she couldn't think of her first impression of him without feeling distinctly unsettled.

Reaching the car, she was hit by a blast of hot air as she opened the door and felt the steering-wheel almost burn her hand as she slid in and sat down. Thank goodness for air-conditioning! She turned her key in the ignition, anticipating the moment when the engine would start to send cooling waves of air onto her face and arms, but instead of the familiar hiccup and purr of the motor starting up, there was only the small click of the key and then silence.

A minute more of trying and checking and trying again confirmed the second, and non-medical, of the afternoon's problems—her car quite definitely wouldn't start.

CHAPTER TWO

'BACK again?' Max Costain said, as she re-entered the office suite through the waiting-room door and headed straight for the nearest phone to call the AAA.

Dr Weir was no longer in evidence, and Max was flipping through a file, while downing a large glass of iced water. Paula coveted the latter desperately. She loved this dry heat, but it certainly made you thirsty.

'Car won't start,' she told Max tersely. 'Battery's flat. Parking lights were still on. Can't think why! I don't even remember using them this morning in the first place.'

She turned to the phone, then did a double take back at him as he uttered a suppressed yet explosive, '*Hell!* Damn, Paula, I'm sorry, that's got to be my fault...'

'*Your* fault?'

'Yes.' He ran a distracted hand through his hair to scratch the back of his slim neck. 'There was no key to your trunk—'

'Yes, I meant to tell you—'

'And I couldn't find the interior release at first. I was fumbling around on your dash. I must have put those lights on, without realising it. I'm really sorry, Paula.'

'No, don't be,' she told him quickly. There was really something quite...sweet...about such a very masculine man displaying such remorse. It warmed her. She added truthfully, 'And it's as much my fault as yours. I should have told you about the key, and where the trunk release was, and, anyway, you were doing me a favour in the first place.'

'Not much of a favour, bringing in two boxes of

books. It would have taken you less time than it's going to take you to…what? Call the AAA?'

'I was about to, yes.' She nodded.

'Don't,' he said with authority. 'It's rush hour. They may take an hour or more to get here. Look, I have jumper cables at home. Let me drop you at your place to freshen up a bit while I go pick up the cables. Then I'll buy you dinner. There's a nice little Southwestern place right here next door in the shopping plaza. After that we can jump-start your car and you'll charge up the battery, driving home.'

'No, Max,' she protested. 'I can't ask that of you! All that driving. My place could be miles out of your—'

'It's not,' he told her. 'Brian said you'd bought a place just off San Xavier Boulevard, and I take San Xavier myself. I'm in the San Ysidro foothills, just ten minutes further on from you. It'd be five minutes…' he grinned '…if I drove fast.'

'Which you don't, of course,' she capped, sensing the direction of his humour.

'Not any more. It's funny. Something happens when you turn forty.' He shook his head in mock confusion.

Forty. He was forty. She didn't know why she was surprised. No, she amended to herself, it wasn't surprise. It was the realisation that at forty he must surely be married or somehow seriously involved.

'And as to dinner,' she blurted, 'won't your wife…? I mean…' She trailed off. It sounded like a probe, an attempt to assess his status, and it was. With a perversity that she understood in herself very well, she knew she would feel happier about this if he was married.

He wasn't. This information was presented to her with a flourish of his ringless left hand and a laconic comment, 'No wife.'

'Not every man wears one,' she pointed out a little defensively, 'even in our generation.'

'I did,' he conceded. 'But the tan line it made disappeared well before the divorce was finalised.'

'Oh. OK.' So he was divorced.

Well, so was she.

'Does that make you feel better?'

No, it makes me feel worse.

She didn't say it, of course. Instead, briskly and sensibly she said, 'Yes, I'd hate to think you were keeping someone waiting at home because you felt you owed me dinner. You *don't* owe me dinner, Max.'

'Well, I do, but I sense we could argue about that all night. Would it help if I said I'd just *like* to take you to dinner?'

No, it wouldn't, but how surly she would sound if she admitted *that!* Paula was far too well brought up for such betraying honesty.

'That would be very nice.' She painted on the smile that Chris had learned to see through after a scant year of their eight year marriage, and was horrified to learn from Max Costain's expression, and his drawled words, that he had seen through it in less than a day.

'And you'd accept a cup of poison from me, wouldn't you, if you thought that politeness required it?' he suggested with an evil smile.

'I—I didn't mean to be so transparent.'

'Then you'll have to practise a bit more in front of your mirror,' he advised mildly, and when at this she became positively *hunted* in her body language he laughed and said, 'Relax! If you don't want dinner...if you have other plans...then say so. I just didn't want *you* to think it was an obligation for *me,* that's all.'

Suddenly she was thoroughly impatient with herself. What on earth was she protecting herself against? If she couldn't even accept a casual dinner invitation—one, moreover, that was meant principally as an apology—from a man, without freezing up, then that wasn't healthy and she had better do something about it.

'I'm sorry, Max,' she said with humble sincerity. 'I've been very awkward and difficult about this, haven't I? Dinner would be really nice, and especially Southwestern food. You'll have to encourage me to be adventurous and try something quite new.'

'I should think that anything you could have at Cactus Flower will be new because the chef is pretty experimental in his definition of Southwestern food.'

They talked about food until they reached his car, which was a comfortable but not ostentatious Japanese model in cool white, parked very near her own forlorn machine. It was, as he had said a few minutes ago, rush hour, and his progress up San Xavier Boulevard towards the spectacular red-brown silhouette of the San Ysidro Mountains that walled the north of the city was much slower than the opposite journey she had made this morning had been.

After twenty minutes she finally said, 'Turn left here.' Five minutes later he had turned into her semi-circle of driveway and deposited her at her front door.

'Forty minutes?' he suggested, and she nodded, feeling far more pleasure than she had expected at the thought of going out again. Something new. Something to do. Someone interesting. She *wasn't* going to feel scared or confronted about it!

She didn't change, just added the perfume and jewellery which she found too much of a distraction during the working day—Arpège, a necklace of fine rhinestones and delicate gold chain, and a filigreed gold bracelet that Chris had given her years ago. She renewed her make-up, too, making it a touch heavier, and exchanged low white sandals for heeled Italian leather pumps that would have had her calves and lower back protesting if she'd worn them at the office for ten hours at a stretch.

Theoretically, these simple touches shouldn't have taken almost forty minutes but somehow they did, and Max had pulled the plaited rope handle of the rustic mission bell beside the front door while she was still in the kitchen, drinking another of the long glasses of water which she much preferred to a constant intake of tea, coffee and carbonated drinks.

This meant that Paula had to open the door to him, instead of meeting his car in the driveway as she'd intended, and to have him enter her house, even briefly, felt so much like an invasion that, again, she had to question her response.

If I *should* invite him in for a drink, she decided, flustered, then I don't care. I don't want to!

She just slipped past him, therefore, waited for him to follow her, then ducked back to close the door behind him, all of which had him watching her with an amused twinkle in his eye.

Yes, OK, so she was darting around like a nervous bird!... Or was the twinkle about something else?

She cocked her head. 'It's not possible that I have spinach between my teeth at this stage of the evening so...'

'Just wondering what you've done to yourself, that's all,' he said. 'I'd swear that was the same outfit that Dr Nichols has been wearing all day to dispense medical wisdom to her parade of patients, and yet something is definitely different and this is a very *soignée* Paula I'm seeing now.'

'There's no magic to it,' she told him drily, then listed on her fingers, 'Shoes, perfume, jewellery, make-up, comb, toothbrush.'

'Ah,' he murmured, 'to have the illusion so totally shattered, and so poetically too!'

'Sorry,' she drawled.

She wasn't sorry at all, of course. Flirting was not on the menu. She hadn't yet *quite* concluded that flirting was what he was doing, but she wasn't prepared to take the chance. Whatever it was, it would be rubbed off the blackboard. In that area, as she'd decided five years ago, the kitchen was definitely closed.

He seemed to take the hint, and was quite silent as they got into his car.

'You, uh, didn't forget the jumper cables, did you?' she hazarded a little tentatively, hoping that he wasn't as close to forgetting the original point of this exercise as she was.

'In the trunk,' he answered, and was silent again until finally, after several minutes, he said, 'Funny how the harder you try to think of something to say...'

She laughed and agreed, then blurted something absurd about the colour of the San Ysidro Mountains at sunrise, right on top of his launch into the subject of her interest in children's allergies, so that they both stopped abruptly, both laughed this time and both began again at exactly the same moment.

This time, *he* agreed about the sunrise on the mountains, and *she* began to expound her view that a pediatrician needed to be well versed in the area of allergy. They stopped even more abruptly and gave up the attempt in total despair.

'So...' he theorised after a helpless minute, 'are we to conclude that we're in agreement about both mountain sunrises and children's allergies?'

'Well, sunrises aren't very controversial,' she countered, 'so that's probably a safe bet. Allergies, on the other hand...'

'Controversial in the extreme,' he agreed. 'I ought to warn you, I'm fairly conservative in my approach.'

'Warn me? Do you get the impression I'm part of the lunatic fringe who credits every symptom to an allergic response?'

'It's a very convenient grab-bag.'

'I don't like grab-bags. In fact, that's precisely why I try to keep as informed as possible about the field. It's my responsibility to the kids I see *not* to follow the lead of some parents in blaming ''allergies'' for what can be just bad or lazy child-rearing.'

He looked across at her as he stopped at a traffic light, and his raised eyebrows told her she'd been getting perhaps a little too indignant on the issue, especially in view of the fact that he seemed to agree with her.

What was it about this man? She had to wonder. He kept drawing responses from her that required careful course correction and disconcerting inner questions about her own behaviour. She wasn't normally like this with a new acquaintance, was she? So, what was it?

By the end of their meal, she had an answer...

The food was dazzling and delicious, full of Southwestern ingredients like poblano chillies, avocado, corn, black beans and crunchy tortilla chips, yet the food made far less of an impression than the man. Their conversation moved seamlessly from allergies in children to their mutual experience of children in general. He was an uncle, it turned out, but not a father, while she had to confess to being an only child.

'My parents would have had more,' she told him, 'but my mother became ill and died when I was six. Breast cancer.'

Which wasn't something she normally found herself telling a man about the first time she went out with him. Not that this was 'going out' in the accepted sense of the term, she reminded herself quickly. And he was a medical colleague. She could mention something as confronting as breast cancer and get just this right reaction of a quiet nod of sympathy from him, instead of an appalled hiss or an overly abrupt change of subject or a catechism of insensitive questions—each of which were reactions she'd had in the past from others.

Max Costain didn't need to ask questions. He would know about what her mother's death must have meant to her at the time, what it still meant and what it implied.

Real knowledge, too, not scary half-truths gleaned from sensationalising news stories.

'Anyway,' she went on, 'my father didn't marry again until I was sixteen, and by then Liddy, my wonderful stepmother, was too old to have children of her own. So I guess I became a pediatrician because I didn't know anything about kids,' she finished.

It was a punch line she'd used before. Not particularly funny. Not particularly true. To her surprise, he pounced on it.

'Don't say that! You *do* know about kids!'

'How can you know that?'

'Because Brian says so, for one thing.'

'And you trust Brian's judgement in everything?'

'When it's immediately confirmed by my own,' he returned, studying her lazily. And that was when she knew what her problem with him was. It had been humming between them all day like wind through wire.

Chemistry. Sexual chemistry, of a kind she hadn't felt since the early days with Chris fourteen or fifteen years ago. Her gaze was magnetically drawn to his tanned fingers, caressing the curved bowl of his wineglass, then to the equally tanned column of his throat. He swallowed, and she watched the movement of his Adam's apple, which was just prominent enough to suggest his masculinity but not so much that it impeded the strong lines of his neck.

She felt the strength of her body's instinctive, unwanted response to him like a drug, and was totally aware that what emanated from him—*his* awareness of *her*—was even stronger, and he wasn't troubling to disguise it.

Perhaps that's why I'm feeling it, she thought. Because this isn't how I normally react to a man, even one as attractive as Max Costain. I shouldn't have had that wine when I drink so rarely these days. Oh, God, and he knows, too! I can see it. I've betrayed it somehow before I even knew I was feeling it. If only I'd been more on my guard!

Helplessly she listened to him flirting with her, heard her own definitely provocative replies. She felt the way she was leaning forward in her seat, resting her chin on her hand, felt the unusual creaminess of her smile and knew that her eyes must be sparkling and her cheeks pink.

In him, too…

She saw his grey gaze growing smokier, heard the new husky, caressing note in his dark voice and the confident release of his laughter. At the same time she felt the contradictory tightness of fear building in her, warring with her stimulated senses, until finally, when the waiter had removed their empty plates, she burst out, 'Please stop this!'

'Stop what?'

He knew. He knew quite well, but clearly didn't believe she meant it.

'Stop flirting with me!'

'Well, I will if you will,' he drawled at once smiling, still not taking her seriously—and she could hardly blame him for that! 'What would you like to do instead?' he finished teasingly.

'No.' She shook her head and stiffened in her seat. Gone was the smile and the bright, inviting dazzle in her eyes. 'Don't! I really mean it,' she insisted. 'I find it…very inappropriate.'

'I had the impression you were rather enjoying it,' he challenged lightly, lifting his head. The lights of the restaurant glinted dark gold against his hair. 'Like a tennis match between equally skilled opponents.'

'I was,' she was able to admit. 'It's…been a long time, actually. But don't you think it's so short-sighted…stupid, even…to jeopardise our long-term future as professional colleagues for the sake of the short-term gratification of—of—'

'An affair?' he suggested.

Paula shook her head decisively. 'Oh, no! This evening stops *way* short of an affair, Max!'

'Believe it or not, I wasn't actually so stereotypically male as to be calculating my odds of *that,*' he said, equally decisively. 'I was simply being fairly open about the fact that I've been enjoying your company...your whole presence, actually. At the office today, too. The way that silky skirt swished a little when you walked down the corridor between patients. Your voice, talking to Brian at the coffee-station while I was writing up notes in my office. The way you can't seem to keep your stethoscope from getting mixed up with your hair.'

He spread his hands. 'But if that's offensive...'

'No, *not* offensive,' she clarified spiritedly. 'Really. Let's not make this into a huge *thing,* OK? I simply feel—'

'That it's inappropriate.' He nodded. 'Then that's all you need to say. I'm not the type to—'

'I'm sure you're not,' she came in hastily. 'Please don't think that I've got that impression. That you're a womaniser.'

'God, that's an awful word!'

'It is,' she agreed, 'so why don't we change the subject? And, please, just forget that this whole conversation—'

'And the previous one? The flirting one?'

'Yes. That it ever took place.'

And at that point Max did change the subject, with a smoothness and humour that she could only admire and be grateful for, sketching out for her benefit the seething hotbed of differing opinions on the subject of the current state of coaching in Zuma's best-known university basketball team. She would never have expected to find college athletic department politics so intriguing.

As a subject of discussion between consenting adults,

too, it was definitely safe. Paula began to enjoy herself again…

He didn't, however, suggest dessert.

Several minutes later he conducted the real business of the evening with swift skill, clipping the leads of his jumper cables onto the two terminals of her battery and to the counterparts on his, then starting his engine smoothly so that hers ignited as well. She was left feeling rather helpless and with a determination to acquire a set of jumper cables of her own, as well as a spare battery.

She was also far more aware than she wanted to be of the shape and movement of his body, the tight stretch of twill fabric across his male behind as he bent beneath his car hood and the fall of his syrup-gold hair over his forehead.

'Run it for a few minutes,' he suggested when the engine was idling well, leaning down to her open driver's side window. 'Then we'll head off.'

'You don't have to wait,' she told him, unnerved by his face just a foot from hers.

'What if you happened to stall on your way out of the parking lot?' he pointed out. 'You wouldn't have enough charge yet to restart it. Under such circumstances, wouldn't the sight of my tail-lights as I roared off into the night be a frustrating one?'

'Yes,' she conceded. 'It would. OK. Follow me home.'

And the fact that he ignored the very obvious opportunity for a *double entendre* offered by these last words told her that he'd taken her seriously on the subject of flirting.

She ought, quite definitely, to have been more grateful for this fact than she was. She *was* grateful—very—for the fact that he now turned away from her car window, detached the leads and went to his own car.

He didn't follow her when she turned off San Xavier

Boulevard, just beeped his horn, waved and drove on, so she arrived home alone…still thinking about him, if she was honest…to find it was nine o'clock already. Later than she would have thought.

Switching on the television for some company, and even more for distraction, she heard Channel Six's quite startlingly perky Kelly Rainer, previewing the eleven o'clock news, and wasn't particularly impressed by the news team's view of what constituted the day's most compelling events. Channel Eight didn't have much drama either, but at least there was a movie to follow the brief sound bite of news.

Paula left the television on and went to the kitchen to make some herbal tea. She was tired. She'd been up since before six. Really, she could go straight to bed, and yet she somehow knew she wouldn't sleep yet. The day…and Max Costain…had been too disturbing, and she needed some kind of grounding, some way to get things back in perspective.

I could call Chris, she thought, but immediately dismissed the idea.

It was after eleven in New York. Not that her ex-husband would be asleep. Far from it. He'd be out, at the theatre or a late dinner with theatre friends, the sort of schmoozing that was essential to success in that world, and he wouldn't be home, probably, until the early morning hours.

This was one of the things that had made their youthful, starry-eyed marriage so impossible in the end. She'd risen early, he'd risen late. She'd studied hard—constantly, at home, alone—while he'd been out until all hours with an ever-changing cluster of would-be actors and singers. She'd needed to stay in Ohio to finish college, then medical school, then internship and pediatric residency. He'd needed to be in New York, where the action was and the success stories happened.

For a while they'd tried to make a long-distance marriage work, but in the end it hadn't. Initially, there had been frequent phone calls and weekends together, whenever they'd possibly been able to. She'd flown to New York, sometimes for a single night. He'd reported his gargantuan phone bills to her with a perverse relish. Thirty-seven phone calls to Ohio in a single month! It had added up!

Then the weekends had got less frequent. The phone bills had got lower. They'd drifted apart. It had been quite mutual, never unpleasant, just a little sad, and more than a little arid and unsatisfying in the end. They'd enquired with feigned enthusiasm about each other's doings, like old friends who hadn't seen each other for too long.

Neither had wanted to be the first one to mention divorce. Both had been intensely relieved when much shared skirting around the subject had finally brought it into the open. They'd both agreed that they had been too young, their goals had been too different, they hadn't thought it through enough in advance. Ironically, once the divorce had been finalised they'd enjoyed each other more and had still called each other every few months, though they hadn't actually met in...what, could it really be four years?

Seven years last November since the divorce—that was easy—but *four* years since she'd seen Chris?

I'll call him on Sunday at noon or so, Arizona time, when he'll be home and just waking up, she decided. I'll tell him how well I'm doing here.

And I won't tell him about Max Costain, even though he'll ask about men as he always does... This thought train led along a familiar path and almost had her deciding not to call Chris on Sunday after all.

I don't need to hear it all again. I know he means it, he's quite sincere in those pep talks he gives me, but he's *wrong!* Most men *couldn't* look past it. Already being in a happy marriage with a man when it happened would be different. Something strong and established and well rooted would be able to survive and even grow stronger under such circumstances, but to enter a new relationship...?

How many men could look past it? How many men would want to touch me, sleep with me, when one of my breasts is gone?

That night, when Paula finally slept, dreams seemed to chase her for hours, the same ugly, frightening dreams she'd been having—with lessening frequency, thank goodness—for over five years now.

It had been five years last November since that dreadful day in the shower when she had focused on her left breast properly for the first time in several months and realised that what she'd vaguely dismissed as starting to get the lumpiness that came and went with many women's menstrual cycles had been something far more sinister—a rock-hard mass almost three inches long.

There had been no excuse for the fact that she, a doctor, fully aware of her risk factors and knowing that her own mother had died of the disease in her thirties, had not been performing breast self-examinations monthly. It hadn't been that she'd *never* done them, but with the pressure of her medical training and the stress of her divorce exactly two years earlier, amicable though it had been...

Well, the excuses that weren't excuses kept piling up. She just forgot, that was all, or remembered at the wrong time of the month when hormonal changes could have made any abnormality too hard to detect anyway. Admittedly, too, she was frightened when she did examine her breasts—frightened, when she remembered the trauma of her mother's death, of what she might find.

At least when she *did* find it, that day in the shower, she reacted rationally, making a doctor's appointment at once, following through on his recommendation of an immediate biopsy, then a modified radical mastectomy and follow-up chemotherapy.

She decided against reconstructive surgery. A cloud of questions was beginning to appear at that stage over the safety of silicon implants, which put her off, and there was a psychological component to her decision as well.

'The lump itself seemed like an invader to me,' she told her stepmother, Liddy, while still recuperating from the surgery. 'I think I'd feel that a breast implant would be the same. Something *in* me that wasn't a *part* of me.'

'You always have tended towards the natural rather than the artificial,' Liddy answered, with her usual thoughtful good sense, 'so I can see why you would feel that way. You never even wanted to get your ears pierced, I remember, even when most of your friends did...and your stepmother!'

'I know.' Paula smiled faintly. 'Your earrings are lovely but, no, I've never liked the idea. And my breasts aren't large. It isn't as if I'll be horribly lopsided without a breast implant.'

The attempt at humour was a little close to the bone for both of them, and the subject of breast reconstruction wasn't spoken of between them again. Paula was happy with her decision at the time, and was still happy with it. She also knew that reconstructive surgery remained a possibility any time she changed her mind.

But something else had been removed by the surgery—a confidence in her own sexual identity—and she was perceptive enough about herself to know that a cosmetically created breast, no matter how skilfully done, would not magically restore that.

She had had an eight year marriage, sexually satisfying for several years, and it had ended. It seemed very likely that her years with Chris were her apportioned lot in this department, and in the five cancer-free years since her surgery, while doing everything she could for her health with diet and lifestyle, she had constructed a life for herself without that element—as carefully as a plastic surgeon would have constructed a breast without breast tissue and a nipple from the skin behind her ear.

The dreams came though—several variations on a theme. Sometimes they weren't, on the surface, about cancer or her lost breast at all. In her waking moments she preferred not to dwell on the details or analyse them too closely, but she knew, nonetheless, that they signified a playing out of all her fears. With the treatment she'd had, her vigilant self-examinations and twice-yearly check-ups now, and her careful attention to diet and lifestyle, it was unlikely that she would lose her remaining breast, but evidently her subconscious didn't know that!

Or perhaps it's not the loss of another breast I'm rehearsing in the dreams, she reflected the next morning as she faced the day, feeling washed out and unsettled after an early waking. Perhaps it's the other things I've lost. Like the love of a man and the prospect of a child.

And if I hadn't responded so stupidly to Max Costain last night, hadn't let down my guard like that, I wouldn't have stirred all this up when everything else was feeling so good...

CHAPTER THREE

PAULA had expected to feel horribly embarrassed at her first encounter with Max after last night but, to her immense surprise, she didn't. Not that she could take the credit for this herself. It was all Max.

She had arrived at Catalina Canyon Pediatrics early—to stay on top of things in the new environment, she told herself, but, of course, it was only partly that. A deeper truth was that she wanted to stay on top of the situation—God, was Max Costain's effect on her a *situation* already? By arriving before him, now that she had her own keys to the practice, she could stake out the territory, so to speak.

Accordingly, she had been standing at the coffee-station, drinking a long glass of water after reviewing her morning's appointments, when he breezed in after a hospital round, tipped a wink and a brief greeting to Melissa at Reception, then came past to ask her laconically, 'Car start OK this morning?'

'Yes, no trouble at all.' She just had time to answer before he disappeared into his own office. He emerged again a moment later.

No, 'emerged' was an exaggeration. *Parts* of him emerged—an elbow to lean against the doorway, a solid bracket of hip to rest his hand on and a cheerful expression. 'Got a patient I'd like to talk to you about—later, when you've got a moment.'

'Sure.' She smiled back.

'How about after lunch, ten minutes before we start again?' he suggested.

'Sounds good.'

And that was that. Easy. Friendly. Totally unembarrassing. Quite unselfconscious on both sides. She felt the most wonderful surge of relief and a return to the zesty and contented optimism which had underpinned this move to Arizona from the beginning. Life *was* good.

It looked good, too, for the mother of her first patient that morning, Callie Herbert, although the patient herself, eight-year-old Elizabeth, was clearly not so cheerful.

'She's had this vomiting and diarrhoea since Sunday night,' Mrs Herbert said. 'I'm sure it's just a gastric virus but, with the baby due on Friday…' She patted her large, hard abdomen, and her joyful anticipation of the coming baby was very obvious in the lighting up and softening of her face.

'Poor Elizabeth,' Paula said to the wan-faced and listless girl. 'I guess you don't want to be feeling like this when your new—'

'Brother,' Mrs Herbert supplied. 'We know it's a boy. Thomas.'

'When Thomas arrives.'

'No,' Elizabeth managed, but that was all.

'Poor darling. She hardly slept,' Mrs Herbert said. 'I just thought, though, that I ought to make sure it's nothing more serious, and that she's not dehydrated.'

Paula asked several questions about the onset and nature of the symptoms and whether there was anything else going on, then she examined Elizabeth and found that everything pointed to just what Callie Herbert had suggested—the sort of self-limiting gastric complaint that would have the child feeling weak and listless for the rest of the day and almost back to normal by tomorrow.

'You're right to be concerned about her fluid intake, though,' she told Mrs Herbert finally. 'Have you had her on an electrolyte solution?'

'No.' Mrs Herbert made a face. 'I didn't have any on

hand, and Mike's away till tonight. She was feeling so bad yesterday I didn't want to drag her out to the store, but I'll stop on the way home and pick some up.'

'And reintroduce solid food and other liquids gradually as she seems better,' Paula said. 'Nothing greasy or rich.'

'Well, we're pretty concerned about diet anyway,' Mrs Herbert said.

Blonde Elizabeth began to put her purple top back on and Paula prepared to leave the examining room. 'I bet you can't wait for the baby,' she said to Mrs Herbert as she freed her hair from one end of her stethoscope.

'People say that,' Callie Herbert said with a nod, 'but we waited so long for him...so long to conceive him...that at this stage I'm far more patient than I expected to be.'

Fertility problems? Paula wondered as she left the room. She didn't remember this being noted on Elizabeth's chart so evidently the trouble had developed after the eight-year-old's birth. That happened, and Mrs Herbert looked to be about forty now, which meant that her fertility had probably started to decline even further. No wonder she had patted her tummy so lovingly, then. The unborn Thomas was clearly an intensely wanted child.

Most children in this practice were. It was situated in a neighbourhood of prosperous stores and businesses and comfortable, well-appointed dwellings, which meant that economic considerations certainly weren't a factor in people's decisions to bring children into the world. After lunch, though, Paula was reminded that people had reasons other than financial ones for being ambivalent about a child's impact on their lives.

'This patient of mine,' Max said, swinging absently from side to side on the swivel chair at his desk. 'Four years old... One of those kids your heart just goes out to. Kind of ugly.'

'Ugly?'

'You know...' He spread his hands. '*Not* the kind that silly mothers want to dress in cute outfits and coo over. He's small and he moves awkwardly, he's shy and unconfident, his ears stick out and his teeth are funny.'

'I love him already!' Paula said, not quite sure where Max was going on this.

'So do I...and so does his mother, only he's such a *palpable* disappointment to her. Only child, late child. She and her husband are both high-powered real estate brokers. She wants a quick fix.'

'To what?'

'To everything about Mickey that makes her uncomfortable. The fact that his speech and motor development are average at best. The fact that he's scared of dogs and clowns and loud noises. The fact that he gets bored if she takes him to work with her.'

'Which one might have thought—'

'That approximately ninety-eight per cent of four-year-olds would be bored by? Exactly! And now she's fixed on allergies as the root of the problem.'

'Specific ones?'

'Not that the very well-regarded allergist I sent him to could pinpoint. So now she's decided it's a sort of free-floating allergy to practically everything he's in contact with, only she doesn't have the patience or the commitment to really explore that... I mean, theoretically it's a possibility.'

'Only you don't believe that.'

'I don't believe it,' he confirmed. 'If she put him on a proper elimination diet she might come up with something. But *I* can't do that for her, and *she* can't do it if most of his meals are taken on the run at the local hamburger drive-through or pizza carry-out. What she wants is a big magic bullet for him. Why can't we just inject him with a huge allergy shot that will desensitise him to everything at once? Cover all bases, so to speak, and solve everything about him that she sees as a problem.'

'I sense a degree of hostility here, Max,' she said drily, and he laughed.

'I'm not going to give you many points for perception for that one, I'm afraid, Dr Nichols. It's hanging out a mile.'

'And where do I come in?'

'Tell her where to get off?' he suggested hopefully.

'Yes, I passed an exam in that a year ago,' she countered sarcastically.

'Well, you see, I'm just not very good at being rude to women,' he explained gloomily.

'A form of sexism, surely?'

'Could we consider it a relatively *benign* one, though?'

'You seriously want—?'

'I seriously want you to be present at this consult this afternoon, is all. You'll find that I've...uh...persuaded Erica to leave your schedule blank for that particular quarter-hour. Then you can play the newly arrived expert and I can play the old family physician—I met the little guy in hospital the day he was born—and between us perhaps we can convince her that the first step is just to *believe* in him a little more.'

So at three o'clock Dorinda and Mickey Walters came in for their appointment, and Dorinda Walters directed a non-stop monologue at Paula that was part complaint, part mixed-up allergy theory and part painful, upside-down expression of love for her awkward little boy, while Max got down on his haunches and chatted to Mickey as the latter examined a basket of toys on the floor.

He was definitely an odd-looking little fellow, all elbows and knees and sticking-out ears, with reddish hair and a liberal spattering of freckles on his pink, sensitive skin. Not the complexion for this climate but, of course, from a real estate developer's view, the city of Zuma was a boom town.

'What do you want to be when you grow up, Mickey?' Paula heard Max say to the child after a few minutes.

'A guitarist…'

'A guitarist! Wow!' All three adults recognised that it was an unusual choice for a little boy.

'A guitarist! You see?' Dorinda Walters said, breaking off from her angry flow, as if this was another clear-cut symptom of *something*. 'Geez, Mickey, where do you *get* these crazy ideas?'

He didn't answer, just turned back to the toy truck he'd been pushing and pushed it some more, but mechanically this time, as if he wasn't really thinking about it. When Max switched to asking him about how he felt, he said softly that his throat hurt and his eyes stung.

'You *see,*' Mrs Walters said again. 'And look at him! He's sniffing now, wiping his hand up his nose. I *hate* that! If he's getting another cold, I think I'll kill him. He's always playing on the floor in the most out of the way corners he can find—under desks, under the bed, even—and if I give him a tissue he *leaves* it under the desk so that I find it later or, worse, if we're at the office a *client* finds it. I mean, geez!'

The little session went on for a few minutes more in this vein until Max finally straightened and said pleasantly, 'We need to get him weighed and measured now, which the nurse will do, Mrs Walters. Then Dr Nichols and I will be back to…er…assess all that, and suggest a course of action.'

'Action! That's what I want, for sure!'

In Max's office, Paula looked at him. 'Could all this allergy business be that he's just *crying?* I mean, tight throat, red eyes, runny nose… Crying but trying not to let it show?'

Max spread his capable hands. 'Can you see her accepting that?'

'No!'

'And, anyway, I think there's more to it. You heard what she said about him playing on the floor in out-of-the-way corners. Even the best-cleaned house or office collects dust faster in those areas.'

'Hence more sneezing.'

'So we could conclude that there *is* an allergy to something in the dust. Tests don't always pick it up.'

'Or we could ask ourselves why he hides away like that to play, exposing himself to dust in a way that he wouldn't if he played in the middle of the kitchen floor or wherever.'

'And answer that question fairly quickly. Because he just doesn't feel relaxed and free enough to lay claim to any more open space.'

'Do you know what I *really* think, Max?' she came in. 'Speaking as someone who's new to the practice and hasn't known him since he was one day old...'

'Yes?'

'I think it's beyond our scope. Her lack of acceptance of him runs pretty deep. I'd suggest counselling, in conjunction with some strategies that she'll find less threatening, such as, well, diet, but you don't seem to hold out much hope there. And setting up better play places for him that are kept properly dust-free.'

'Counselling,' Max echoed slowly. 'Yes, I think it *has* got to that point. She needs to see how her interactions with him are making everything worse, and that's just not our role. Sometimes the medical part of the problem is just the tip of the iceberg, isn't it?'

'I had one like that yesterday,' Paula replied, and told him about the teenage boy with *grand mal* seizures, Sam Hasher. 'I'm wondering if he actually *needs* them for some reason.'

'Or if he's even inducing them,' Max suggested.

'There was a kid in my class when I was about ten who did it to entertain us a couple of times—until our teacher and his parents persuaded him what a bad idea it was. He'd lie on the floor and look up at the ceiling fan in the cafeteria, which had a bright fluorescent light above it, and when one of us turned off the fan and it slowed to just the right speed—bingo! The strobe effect would bring on a seizure. Since he thought it was funny, so did we.'

'Inducing them,' Paula murmured thoughtfully. 'You know, I wonder... Thanks, Max, I'm going to think about that when I see him next week.'

'Thank *you,* Dr Nichols.' He smiled crookedly. 'For fending off Dorinda Walters while I listened to Mickey, which she's never really given me the chance to do before. A guitarist! There's a really sensitive little soul in that funny little guy. I *am* going to suggest counselling, and we'll see what develops. I can deal with it myself now.'

'Glad I could help,' she told him, meaning it.

Aside from what her own small contribution might ultimately mean to the awkward little boy, she had relished finding out more about her senior partner's rapport with children, and had been both impressed and warmed. Max Costain had looked completely at home down there on the floor with the toys, despite his impressive height and build.

And it's easy for most people to relate well to a cute kid, Paula realised. I mean, who couldn't? But to relate well to the odd ones, or the ugly ones, or the sullen ones, or the ones who throw tantrums...

Within the next ten days she glimpsed Max skilfully at work with each of these types and more, and by the end of that time the gradual, frightening knowledge had crept up on her that her attraction to him was growing.

It wouldn't have happened, perhaps, if he'd flirted with her as blatantly as he had that first night, but he *didn't* flirt with her...or, if he did, it was so subtle and charming that she interpreted it merely as friendliness, which indeed it probably was. By the time she realised the stark fact that she was very disturbingly starting to want more than friendliness, and that friendliness was, therefore, perhaps far more dangerous than flirting would have been, it was too late.

Now didn't *that* all sound horribly confusing and contradictory?

'And what am I going to do about it?' she demanded aloud of herself on Friday morning. 'Nothing...nothing. It will go away. Thank goodness I put him off that first night because now that he's sure I'm not interested he's too considerate to try again, which is lucky because if he did I might respond and that would be...impossible! Oh, let it go away!'

Parking in the doctors' parking area at the hospital, a scant few minutes' drive from the practice, she realised that another doctor, a stranger to her, had just parked in the adjoining space and had caught sight of her solitary mutterings at the steering-wheel.

OK, yes, so I'm going crazy, she conceded, but this time she avoided alarming the poor man even further by keeping the words safely inside her own head.

It was the last day of the working week, her second in the practice, and she was here to visit baby Thomas Herbert, Callie Herbert's new little son who had been born just last night, several days late. She would check him in the nursery first, look at his chart to see what the hospital pediatric resident had said about his delivery, then go and report to Callie herself on what she had seen.

There was only one hitch to this plan. Baby Thomas wasn't in the nursery.

'His mother's feeding him,' one of the nurses said. 'We told her you'd probably be here in a minute but he was crying so she didn't want to wait.'

'That's all right,' Paula told him cheerfully. 'I'll pop

down to her now and say hi, then wait. At this stage, she won't be giving him a half-hour feed.'

She got the number of Callie Herbert's room and went along the corridor, her tread silent on the thick carpet so that when she reached the door, which was a foot or two ajar, and slipped through it Callie didn't hear her.

She was absorbed in feeding the baby, the dark, downy little head held against her left breast, which was not yet engorged with milk but much enlarged, nonetheless, from the hormonal changes of pregnancy. Paula couldn't help watching in silence for a moment. Such a lovely picture! Callie's smile, her straight caramel-coloured hair falling around her face, the pretty white and mauve floral nightgown that she'd obviously bought especially for this hospital stay.

There was something odd, though, something not quite right. Callie's left breast was large and full, but the right… The lacy yoke of the nightgown fell there with just a gentle curve to her still-protruding abdomen. There was no engorgement of her right breast at all.

It shouldn't have been such a shock. Paula knew that there were women who conceived, bore and breastfed babies after they had had breast cancer, but it was a rare enough thing that she hadn't encountered it personally during her own years of practice. Because her feelings about her own cancer were a little raw and confronting at the moment, she found it unbearable to look and fled back in the direction of the nursery, her heart beating fast, her breathing shallow and her hands clammy.

Hang on, though! Backtrack a bit, there. She was feeling raw about her breast cancer at the moment? Why? She'd been both cancer-free and without one breast for over five years. Why was it confronting her so freshly *now?*

Because of Max Costain.

She knew it when she saw him standing there in the nursery, examining another new baby who was now a patient of the practice. He must have arrived during the brief interval when she'd stood frozen in the doorway of Callie Herbert's room. Now, she stood frozen again.

He hadn't seen her yet. He was focused on the baby—a girl. Her wheeled, Plexiglas bassinet had a pink card at the head of it, announcing the baby's vital details. He looked at her chart, listened to her chest and heart with a stethoscope, checked her reflexes and looked at her umbilical cord site. Then he checked the mother's room number and turned to leave, and only at this point did he catch sight of Paula.

The absorbed, professional expression dropped from his face and it lit up with his wide, frank smile—which prompted her to immediately add one to her own face just as he came past.

'No,' he said at once. 'I'm afraid you still need quite a bit more practice.'

'I'm...sorry?'

'In the mirror. Your smile. To give it that genuinely sincere quality,' he explained, wickedly serious, and she remembered the way he'd seen through her expression that very first day.

She flushed. 'Oh, I—'

'What's the matter, Paula?' And somehow he had swept her out of the nursery in the current of his own departure.

'Nothing!'

'That's disappointing...'

'What?'

'Well, if nothing's the matter, then the patent insincerity of your smile must mean you weren't pleased to see *me*, and that's...disappointing.'

'Oh, Max... Of course I was pleased to see you!' The tension left her suddenly in a laughing sigh and had her slumping even as she walked beside him, slumping to the point where her fallen shoulder nudged his arm, and a second later she found that the arm—strong and warm—had curved around her, pulling her against him, shoring her up.

'Hang in there,' he said. 'Tired?'

She seized on the word gratefully and because it was true—she *was* tired at the end of a long week—she was able to say with conviction, so that he didn't see through the words to the fact that there was much more, 'Yes, very tired.'

His arm tightened around her, making the silk of her ice-green blouse slip against her skin, and it felt so right that she left it there. His other hand came to spread across her fine hair and pull her head gently down to his shoulder, where she obediently let it rest, helplessly loving the masculine hardness of the pillow of muscled flesh and feeling that electric hum again—awareness. Powerful, prickling on her skin, tingling down her spine, softening her, melting her, making her weak and happy…and scared.

'Max…'

Saying his name was meant to be the adjunct to her pulling away, regaining control, but that part of the plan didn't happen and she stayed so that it became a word of soft encouragement to him, provocation almost, and she felt him turn slightly, bend a little and press his lips to her hair.

'Hang in there,' he repeated, and then he let her go. 'Have you got a minute?'

'I have, actually. My patient is drinking his breakfast. Oh, is this my chance to meet our mother of quads?' Her focus returned to medical matters at once.

'Yes, it'd be a good time. She's been having some pre-term labour but they've settled that down for the moment.'

'Still…'

'I know. It could happen at any time. With something like this, you have to be grateful for every day, and every day increases the chances that all four will make it.'

'Tough on the mother.'

'Very! But she's doing great. Well, you'll see in a minute.'

He led the way to the far side of the maternity floor and they went into a two-bed room to greet a pretty woman of about thirty-three with blonde, wavy hair. Despite a delicate-featured face and slim arms, her body made a mountain in the bed, and she could only sit up higher with the help of a mechanism which could raise or lower the top end of the bed at the touch of a button.

A nurse was with her, just detaching a blood pressure cuff, and Lisa Carey turned immediately from saying hello to the two doctors in order to ask, 'What was it, Althea?'

'One-twenty over eighty,' Nurse Althea Jackson answered, and Lisa nodded, satisfied.

'Pretty good,' Max commented.

'A year ago, you could have told me three hundred over ten and I wouldn't have had a clue,' Lisa said, 'but now… I think I'll start lecturing in maternal-fetal medicine once I'm out of here!'

They laughed, then Max added, 'So how are you?'

'I can tell you in five letters. B-O-R-E-D.'

'I know.'

'S-C-A-R-E-D, too. But…no point in getting stressed. Thanks for dropping in. And you've brought a new face.'

'I have. This is Dr Paula Nichols, the new partner in our practice, who's going to share the load of your four with me.'

'Good! At the birth, too?'

'I certainly plan to be!' Paula said.

'It's going to be crowded, isn't it?'

They chatted for a few minutes more, then Lisa's breakfast—rather large—arrived so they took their departure.

'Was she having fertility treatment?' Paula asked Max as they returned to the nursery and postnatal ward.

'Yes, for just one month. Reading between the lines, I get the impression that her specialist may have jumped in too soon and too aggressively because, although it's an interesting opportunity for us, quads is *not* the desired outcome of fertility treatment. Now, next... Ah, yes! Maria Sifuentes,' he said, 'and she's in this room. Where's yours? *Who's* yours?'

'Oh...' Paula answered vaguely, finding it a struggle to drag her awareness away from Max. 'Callie Herbert. She delivered last night. Routine, vaginal. Everything in the chart looked good, but I haven't seen him yet because, as I said, when I looked in a few minutes ago she was still feeding him. She's probably finished now.'

'See you at the office in a while, then.'

Seconds later he had disappeared into Maria Sifuentes's room, leaving the door just ajar behind him.

Callie Herbert *had* finished feeding baby Thomas. He was asleep, still cradled in the crook of her arm, his head shadowed a little by the weight of her breast in its nursing bra and lacy nightgown above him. She looked up and smiled this time as Paula entered, evidently having expected her.

'Sorry,' she said. 'I looked up before and just saw you disappearing. I've kept you waiting. Are you going to check him now?'

'Yes, and I can do it right here, if you like,' Paula answered. 'But I do need to have him in the bassinet, and he'll probably wake up.'

'That's all right. It's important to know straight away that he really is healthy, isn't it?'

She passed the baby to Paula, who laid him in the bassinet to make her examination.

'He's beautiful, Callie,' she summarised to the happy mother a few minutes later. 'Healthy, a good size, everything as it should be. He fed for you, didn't he?'

'About five minutes. I didn't try for more. I know if he goes too long at this stage I'm likely to get sore, and since...actually... Of course my obstetrician knows all about this—I only have one useful breast these days, Dr Nichols. I don't think I've mentioned it to you or Dr Hunt.'

'No, you're right. It...wasn't noted on Elizabeth's chart that you'd had a breast removed,' Paula agreed quietly.

'Well, I did. A modified radical mastectomy of my right breast when she was just eighteen months old. I breastfed her, too, until she was ten months, and after that I thought for a long time that the lump was related to nursing, or to stopping nursing. I had reconstructive surgery—nothing remotely voluptuous because I was small-breasted to begin with—but, of course, that doesn't mean I can produce milk in that breast. I got very lop-sided as the pregnancy progressed!'

'Welcome to the club!' Paula came in.

'What? You mean...?'

'Yes, I lost my left breast just over five years ago.'

Callie smiled—a rueful smile that acknowledged their shared understanding of what that simple statement involved.

'You'll understand, then,' she responded. 'That's why we waited so long to have Thomas. I wanted to be cancer-free for five years before we risked having another child, and we've all held our breaths through this pregnancy. Some people disapproved of us having another baby at all, "in case you don't live to see him grow up"! That made me so mad! As if any mother is guaranteed that!'

Paula gave a nod of understanding and agreement.

'I think it's wonderful,' she said sincerely. 'Really wonderful!'

Could that have been me? she wondered as she drove from the hospital to the practice a few minutes later. It wasn't the first time she had considered this question. Would her life have been different if she and Chris had still been married when she'd discovered the lump in her breast?

Perhaps it would have brought us closer. Perhaps I might even be in Callie's position now, having a child… But this painfully beguiling fantasy was built on a foundation of quicksand, and she knew it.

It was one of the things she had been most grateful about over the past five years—that her divorce had been amicably settled before cancer had shadowed her horizon. That way, she had never been in any danger of confusing the two issues. They were entirely separate, and she wasn't going to make the mistake of tangling them together now.

CHAPTER FOUR

SAM HASHER was on her appointment list for today, straight after school at four o'clock. He had originally been scheduled for Monday, but his mom had called at the last minute to cancel and suggested today instead.

Paula marked the appointment with an asterisk, which gradually became an intricate and heavily inked doodle in the margin of the computer-printed appointment sheet as she considered the difficult teenager.

She was really going to mine deeper today. There was something going on, a reason for his increasingly frequent seizures that went beyond the physiological, and if she could see him alone...

At first it seemed that luck was with her. Nursing Assistant Vicky Domingo called him in to Exam Room 6 and he was waiting for Paula there alone when she arrived a few minutes later, but being without his mother didn't seem to have put him in the mood to be honest and expansive.

'How is the new stuff?' Paula asked, deliberately casual.

'Oh, it's OK.'

'But has it started to control the seizures?'

He shrugged. 'No...'

Clearly, he knew what was coming next. She said it. 'Let's try a slight increase in the dose, then.'

She was fully aware that she was giving as much of a performance—and a fairly apathetic one, at that—as he was, and she was just about to cut through the thick layer of pretence when the examination room door opened without a warning knock and the man who had to be Sam's father lumbered impatiently in.

The resemblance between the teenager and the older man was unmistakable, but in the former there was a simmering, defeated sort of anger while in the latter the violence was clearly far closer to the surface, far more indiscriminate and far more dangerous.

Paula felt her spine prickle as Ray Hasher demanded in an ugly tone, 'How long does this take? That waiting room is full of screaming kids...'

Which had to be an exaggeration. Catalina Canyon Pediatrics was efficient enough that the waiting room was very rarely full and, as for screaming, there were far too many colourful toys and books to leave children with time for tears.

Sam Hasher threw Paula a pleading look that said, Don't keep me. He's mad about something and I'm the one he'll take it out on.

Paula hesitated. She *really* wanted to go beyond merely upping the dose of Sam's new medication but, frankly, she was almost as intimidated by Ray Hasher as his son seemed to be. Certainly she could send Mr Hasher out to wait again, but it was already obvious that she wouldn't get anything more out of Sam today. Suppressing a sigh, she wrote down the new instructions for his medication and handed the small sheet of paper to him silently.

'Should I make another appointment?' he wanted to know.

'No, Sam,' she said, 'because I'd like to talk to your mom about scheduling it so I'll give her a call, OK?'

'OK.'

'Let's go,' Ray Hasher growled.

He had been rocking to and fro on his heels and glaring around the clean, pleasant little examination room as if it might infect him at a touch, and now he hustled his son out the door with a hard, stiff grip on his shoulder.

Whew! Paula had to stop for a minute to collect herself, but didn't have longer than that as appointment secretary Erica knocked at that moment to ask if Paula could fit in a five-month-old in half an hour. 'Her mother's just picked her up from the sitter and, apparently, she's been crying all day and is really hotting up now.'

'Tell her to come in,' Paula said.

It meant that she had to try and get ahead a little if she could, and didn't have any more time to dwell on the question of Sam Hasher.

After the five-month-old had been seen, however, diagnosed with an ear infection and prescribed an antibiotic, Paula did manage to reach Sam's mother by phone at work and arranged to see him alone for an extended check-up the Monday after next.

'It may take a while,' she stressed. 'Perhaps you could do as we discussed before and fill in the time with shopping?'

She didn't want to be too upfront about what she wanted as she was beginning to sense that, whatever was going on in the family, Mrs Hasher wanted it kept safely under wraps as much as Sam seemed to. Mrs Hasher seemed unsuspicious, though.

This small success brought the day to a close.

Max was just coming past when she closed her office door behind her, and she felt her usual helpless lift of happiness and warmth at the sight of him, coupled with the simultaneous sensations of anticipation and calm which should have been contradictory but somehow weren't.

They smiled at each other, and he would have gone past only something in her expression suddenly seemed to make him hesitate, as if he thought she was about to speak. He *did* think so. His look was questioning. 'Hmm?'

'Sorry. Nothing,' she answered quickly. 'I was just smiling. I—'

'Yes, and much better, too,' he commended her with deliberately exaggerated kindness. 'I can tell you've been practising.'

'No, I haven't,' she stammered. 'I mean, it was a real smile.'

'Awrright!' He pumped a fist in the air. 'I'm getting a *real* smile now! That's got to be progress!'

'Not that—' She collected herself, and drawled deliberately, 'Look, it's really not considered necessary *or* good manners to call attention to those little bits of polite insincerity we all pull from time to time, Max. If we only ever smiled when we felt like it—'

'OK. True,' he conceded judiciously. Then he produced those silvered sunglasses from a pocket somewhere and put them on so she couldn't see his eyes anymore.

It made her uncomfortable, as it always did, so she appended indignantly, 'And, anyway, talking of insincerity, those glasses of yours, which you could be plotting homicide behind and no one would be able to tell—'

'You don't like them?'

'Is this a private fight,' enquired Deborah Weir drily, as she came past, 'or can anyone join in?'

'It's private,' Max answered firmly. 'So private that I didn't realise it *was* a fight. Is it a fight, Paula?'

'Not at all,' she argued, indignant at the idea. Deborah lost interest and passed on so Paula added sternly, 'And I *do* like your sunglasses, only you shouldn't put them on when you're talking to someone or it gives the impression—like my smile, you'd probably claim—that you don't want people to know what you're thinking.'

'Perhaps I don't.'

'If so, a little more subtlety wouldn't go amiss.'

'My sunglasses aren't subtle?'

'Not very, no.'

'Again, like your smile.'

'Oh, dear, we're back to that!'

And they were on their way out of the office suite together, too, which had somehow happened without her conscious assent. There was nothing that she could do about it now, however, and, since there was something perversely pleasant about bickering happily like this, she walked with him down the stairs and through the desert-landscaped courtyard.

They'd stopped bickering now, and suddenly the silence started to feel rather too thick, giving her time to confront this growing feeling in her that Max Costain was already making her question decisions about her life that she'd thought, less than two weeks ago, had been very firmly in place.

She wasn't exactly doing a good job of concealing the fact, either. Maybe *she* needed some silver-lensed sunglasses because he was speaking now, and what was he saying?

'Busy tonight?'

'Sorry?' She'd heard him perfectly well, as it happened, but was so flustered at the immediate realisation that his question was the prelude to an invitation that she needed to buy time.

'I asked if you were busy tonight,' he repeated. 'And, yes, I *do* hope that you'll say you're not.'

'W-why?' she asked inanely.

'Because I got the distinct impression this morning,' he said very deliberately, 'that it might be worth trying again.'

He took her for a picnic up Catalina Canyon, and from the moment he picked her up at her front door she was a helpless and only too willing accomplice in his very open seduction...

No, seduction was too strong a word. Flirtation, perhaps, as he'd attempted ten days ago? No, that wasn't right, either. This was far warmer than a flirtation. It fell, then, somewhere in between, and very soon she stopped trying to label it and even forgot, temporarily, to be frightened of it.

'Have you been up the canyon yet?' he asked her as they drove up San Xavier Boulevard then headed east and north again to where Catalina Canyon began to make its deep gash through the spectacular reddish craggy rock of the San Ysidro Mountains.

'Not yet,' she confessed.

'I guess you were waiting to be guided by a local.'

'I guess I must have been.'

Private vehicles weren't allowed up the single winding road that climbed the bottom of the canyon so Max left his car in the parking lot and they bought tickets on the open, canopied electric shuttle that provided a ride to one of the half-dozen designated stops along the half-hour route.

'There is another way of getting to the head of the canyon,' he told her as he brought a canvas and leather backpack out of his car and swung it onto his shoulders.

'Oh, yes?'

'But we're not taking it so don't even ask!'

'Well, I won't,' she agreed obediently, 'if it's that bad.' She thought a little nervously, Hang-gliding? Abseiling? From the peak of Mount Ysidro itself?

A few minutes later, as they boarded the shuttle, she saw what he meant—joggers. Dozens of them, equipped with the latest in revealing black Lycra shorts, tight midriff-baring tops and portable CD players, some with music audible even through their headphones.

'I'm of the opinion that jogging,' Max said sweepingly, 'is a form of total insanity. Would you agree?'

'I...er...think perhaps I wouldn't dare to disagree!'

'That'll do.'

'I do, though, like to have a good walk fairly often.'

'Now that,' he told her, 'is an entirely different thing,

and, in fact, what I propose today is that we get off at the last stop and walk back, in an energetic yet suitably restrained manner, *down* the canyon to one of the stops midway along, a distance of about two and a half miles. A *civilised* distance, in other words. I mean, that Greek guy…'

'Which guy?' She was completely confused. She couldn't call many 'Greek guys' to mind, off the top of her head. Jackie Kennedy Onassis's deceased husband? Oedipus?

'The one who had to warn whoever it was that somebody was attacking somebody else. Or something.'

'Oh, you mean the *Marathon* guy?'

'That's the guy,' he agreed. '*He* jogged. But he was running to save lives!'

'Or his country, even.'

'His country! Good point!'

'I think it was his country,' she amended, frowning uncertainly.

'City-state? Athens?'

'I guess neither of us took ancient history,' she was forced to conclude.

'Anyway, the point is—'

'The point is, I completely agree with you,' she assured him kindly.

'Good,' he drawled, 'because, in retrospect, I've laboured it a bit, haven't I?'

'Pheidippides,' someone suddenly said from the shuttle seat behind them. It sounded like a sneeze.

They both turned, a little startled.

'The Greek guy,' said an elderly Englishman cheerfully, 'was Pheidippides. A courier sent to Athens to announce the Athenian victory against the Persians at the plain of Marathon in 490 BC. He actually collapsed and died on arrival, although that distance was only twenty-six miles. The time you're thinking of, when he was bringing a warning that saved lives, was somewhat earlier that same year when he ran 150 miles in two days to warn Sparta that the Persians were attacking Athens. Of course, the marathon we know today wasn't actually run in the ancient Olympic games at all.'

'Thank you,' Paula said inadequately. Actually, she felt a little embarrassed. Had everyone in this first car of the shuttle tram heard their discussion about 'the Greek guy'?

'And,' the elderly man continued, 'on the subject of jogging, I'm entirely of your opinion.'

There was a chorus of cheerful assent from all around them.

OK. Everyone *had* heard!

Paula and Max exchanged a very sheepish—and this time hopefully *private*—smile, just as the shuttle set off on its extremely relaxing journey up the canyon.

The female driver gave a chirpy little commentary for the benefit of the tourists aboard, which Paula frankly ignored in favour of simply looking around her at the soaring canyon sides and the saguaro cactuses, with their shapes suggestive of headless men or modern sculpture or contorted dancers, and listened to the rush of the bold little river over the smooth rocks while a wonderful sense of peace and contentment grew in her.

Grew, that was, until she caught the flash of Max's silver sunglasses turned in her direction and realised he wasn't listening to the commentary *or* watching the play of light on the canyon walls, but was watching *her* as if she was a far more intriguing and complex sight.

Surrounded by other people as they were, she didn't dare to react but just looked quickly away again, to a randomly chosen spot behind his right shoulder, as if she hadn't noticed his scrutiny at all. Her heart was pounding, though. What was he hoping to read in her? What was she prepared to give away? What would she manage to keep to herself?

She was more drawn to him every minute but was

terrified to have him know it yet—hadn't thought this through at all. Was she suddenly reneging on every decision she'd made over the past five years? Had she suddenly acquired a faith that a physical relationship with a man *wasn't* so impossible for her after all? And why hadn't she had to face this issue before?

This last was the easiest of the questions to answer: because the men who had expressed an interest in her—and, yes, there had been several—had been far easier to resist than Max. There was just no comparison in that area. In those cases—Matt, Jeff, David—her own body and soul hadn't been playing traitor as they were doing now.

In a flash of belated insight she saw that she'd said no to Matt and Jeff and David not because she'd decided to keep that element out of her life on principle, but because fundamentally each man himself hadn't interested her. There had been no strength of purpose at work there, no commendable acceptance of her own needs and limitations, as she had fooled herself into believing at the time. It had been easy.

This time it wasn't going to be easy at all.

When they climbed from the shuttle twenty minutes later they were suddenly alone. The party of English, Canadian and American tourists that had accompanied them in the shuttle weren't alighting for a more thorough exploration of the canyon but were taking the ride straight back down again.

Higher up on a narrow, rocky trail that zigzagged back and forth across the steep canyon sides was a small group of hikers from an earlier ride up, and about a quarter of a mile down the road they had passed another group who were walking down, as Max and Paula were about to do, but just at this spot there was no one, and that was suddenly such a relief that they both smiled again at once and the dry desert air almost shimmered...like a mirage...with their awareness of each other.

Though early evening now, after six-thirty, it was still quite hot. They both wore sturdy athletic shoes and shorts, his a practical khaki, hers a more frivolous floral in turquoise and white with a matching T-shirt-style blouse. Even so, they probably both would have been sweating a little except that the dry air evaporated any moisture almost instantly from their skin, especially when the capricious breeze chanced to blow their way, cooling them wonderfully.

'Do you want to strike on up the trail a bit?' Max asked, and Paula followed his gaze to the hikers who were already up there, just pale moving dots now, bobbing along the faintly scored line through the dry cactus scrub that was the trail.

'Uh...'

Her hesitation, brief though it was, drew an instant response from him. 'No? Good decision! Let's go.'

He seized her hand and she felt the warm slide of the ball of his thumb across the slender bones of her fingers before his larger palm had totally engulfed them.

It was an exhilarating, easy journey. They walked fast, and the air was so clean and clear and dry that walking felt like floating and her shoes felt as if they had springs.

Twice they crossed the fast, saucy little river and stopped to cool off, by leaving the pale cement road and climbing across the smooth rocks to plunge their hands into the race of the glass-clear water, which was surprisingly cold, and splash their faces and necks.

He had said it was two and a half miles to where they would stop to eat, but it didn't seem like nearly that far. There were other picnickers there when they reached the spot, but there was enough room on the coarse, river-washed sand and enough privacy offered by the scattered stands of low, shrubby trees for them to feel alone.

The picnic was a simple one. 'By virtue of its short

notice,' he pointed out. 'I threw everything into the bag in the space of five minutes because I knew otherwise we'd miss the six o'clock shuttle, which wouldn't have given us much time as they close this place at nine, this time of year. Last tram's at eight-thirty.'

They ate fairly quickly. Crackers and cheese and salami. Fruit and vanilla yoghurt. Lightly flavoured fizzy mineral water. In the heat, anything more would have been too heavy.

Then suddenly the heat was gone, seeping out of the canyon along with the sunshine, which had retreated up to the high rockface now, where it glowed gloriously against the blue sky. The cool stillness was wonderful. Most of the remaining picnickers left on the eight o'clock tram, and a light dew began to fall like a cool blanket.

Paula had taken off her shoes and cotton socks to wade up to her calves in the water, loving its fast, pure flow, but now that began to feel too chilly so she came out of the water and joined Max, who had disdained paddling in favour of exploring upstream on the rocks.

'I expect you thought of the fact that cotton socks would be impossible to get back onto wet feet when you decided against my idea,' she told him, as the chilled flesh of her dripping toes squeaked against the stubborn knit.

'If that's an upside-down request for help...'

'No, it isn't! Really!' she insisted, alarmed.

But it was too late. He sat beside her on the grass and pulled a large, clean white handkerchief from his back pocket, pivoted her legs to rest both her bare wet feet on his tanned thighs and was using the handkerchief like a towel. Paula could only sit back on her hands helplessly, watching him...and feeling the hard, warm curve of his thighs beneath her lower calves and her insteps.

It was a more sensuous moment than she would have believed possible. His fingers kept nudging the sensitive skin of her high insteps, and the rhythmic movement of the handkerchief was like a massage, sending vibrations all the way up her bare legs.

When her feet were almost dry she expected him to stop and turn over the task of putting on the socks to her, but he didn't. Instead, he gathered the stretchy knit folds of each sock between his fingers and thumbs and slid them over each foot, right then left.

It was only as he completed the task that he finally gave a deliberate caress, pushing each sock up each ankle and then sliding his hands further to find the achingly soft hollows behind her knees and tickle them. The teasing movement of his fingers sent electric tingles chasing each other up her spine, and she gave a convulsive shiver that was part ecstasy, part fear.

'I—I can do the shoes. Thanks, Max.'

It came out abrupt, almost gruff, and she was angry at him all at once—angry about how easy it had been for him to produce this powerful effect on her.

And even angrier when he said in a liquid, provocative way, 'You have pretty feet, Paula. No corns, no bunions, no hangnails.'

'So that was what it was all about,' she said shortly. 'An inspection. Of my hooves. Like a thoroughbred horse.'

He seemed startled. 'No, it wasn't! If I carried tissues instead of a handkerchief, I wouldn't have done it.'

She wasn't ready to relent yet. 'And I don't know why you still need your sunglasses. The sun's almost completely gone.'

'You really hate my sunglasses, don't you?' he said.

'Because I can't see what you're looking at,' she pointed out. 'I can't see your eyes.'

'Here, then,' he said, as he very deliberately reached up and removed those ultra-fashionable shades. 'Now you can see my eyes.'

He meant her to look and she did, having no choice

about the matter at all, and she could see immediately what he was looking at. Her. And he wasn't bothering in the slightest to hide the desire that smouldered in those blue-grey depths, either.

'I wasn't inspecting you, Paula, I was…discovering you, and it was every bit as wonderful as I knew it would be. The delicate fineness of your skin, the dusting of those silky little hairs on your calves that are almost invisible. Most women shave them and, frankly, that stubbly effect is a *big* turn-off!'

'I—I—'

She flushed horribly at this. To be complimented for not removing the hair on her legs! She hadn't done so since a few messy experiments with wax and depilatory cream in her late teens because, as he'd said, the hairs there were so fine that they scarcely showed, but it was unorthodox and it underlined the fact that she hadn't imagined she'd have to deal with a man's touch in such a sensitive area.

These days a woman's lower legs were more off limits to a man's hands than…

Her breasts.

He'd caressed her legs and now he was looking at her with raw desire. A kiss came next…and she had to suppress a shudder of need, already able to imagine how searing and skilled his kiss would be. If his fingers could do what they'd just done to her insteps, what would his mouth do to her tender lips?

And breasts came next, as soon as a man dared, perhaps in a schoolboy sort of hope that touching that sizzlingly responsive zone would unlock the key to the whole treasure chest. Only in her case, the very thought of him trying to touch her there…

'Is it so bad, Paula?' Max was saying softly, and there were his fingers again, scooping lightly into the hollows behind her knees, running down to the sleek curves of her calves, making a warm ring of flesh around her slender ankles.

'No.' Somehow she couldn't lie. 'It's very good...'

Then they both heard the engine of the day's last shuttle coming past them on the road, heading up the canyon to the final two stops. It would turn around at the end of the road and come straight back, which meant they only had a few minutes to pack away the picnic things and take the short trail through sand, rocks and streambed growth to their own stop just up the road.

They parcelled up the leftovers in silence, then he shouldered his pack and they walked together away from the river.

Paula was home by a quarter past nine, and the lights she had left on inside before she left beckoned golden through the tinted glass panels beside her mission-style front door.

Just thank him and say goodnight, they seemed to say. There's no need to do more. Make it easy on yourself. It's safe in here...as long as he doesn't come in too.

And yet she ignored the message the lights were sending, and heard herself say...heard the tight, tentative quality to it, as well, 'Come in for a bit? I made a nut loaf last night, and there's coffee. Something stronger, if you'd like it.'

He looked at her for a long moment in the smoky orange light of the streetlamp and finally nodded. 'OK. I will. Thanks.'

The awkwardness between them lasted until the coffee had been made and poured and the rounds of nut loaf sliced, thinly buttered and served. She had told him to choose some music and put it on, and when she came through from the kitchen to her cool, spacious living room, with coffee, loaf and all the fixings on a tray, she was greeted by the sounds of a female country balladeer—and by his grin.

'I like this,' he said, 'but if you think it's a bit over the top...'

'It's in my collection, isn't it?' she pointed out. 'It *is* over the top! I love it!'

'It could have been a gift,' he countered, 'which you'd been too polite to get rid of. I like it, too. Over-the-topness has its place.'

'And tonight is part of that place?'

'Maybe,' he said cryptically. 'Can't...make up my mind on that.'

It was a threat of sorts, and they both knew it. He was biding his time, and he continued to do so as they ate, drank and talked. Paula kept thinking in a panicky way, Why did I do it? Why did I ask him in? The *signals* that sends! Not that a man like Max is going to interpret it crudely and single-mindedly, as a lot of men might, but even so...

And he did kiss her. Was there ever any doubt that he would? Was there ever any doubt, either, that he'd manage it beautifully, with a mixture of beguiling boyishness, adult confidence and real tenderness that came by instinct, not by learning or even by experience?

Knowing it was coming, Paula had her own response precisely calibrated and at the ready. She would return his kiss—warmly, sincerely, but briefly—then would firmly pull away and tell him the lines she'd busily rehearsed during a brief break in the bathroom.

Sort of rehearsed, anyway!

She hadn't been able to strike quite the right chord in her mind, but contented herself with the theory that a bit of spontaneity and ad-libbing was likely to work better, in any case. Something, though, along the lines of finding him attractive, and so on, obviously, not in any way wanting to suggest...blah, blah...she'd fill in something there...but she just wasn't looking for any kind of commitment...no, any kind of *relationship*...at all at the moment so it would be best if…whatever…they didn't see each other outside of…blah, blah.

When it did come, though—Max's kiss—every bit of this hazy and well-intentioned plan evaporated completely.

His mouth on hers was magic, capturing her lips with gentle, teasing movements at first so that she sighed and lifted her face and let her own mouth cling and open and begin to explore. Oh, she hadn't done this…hadn't *felt* this…for so long.

Perhaps she had *never* felt this, not exactly this. Because there was a complexity to her feelings now that hadn't been there in her early twenties with Chris. She knew what it could mean to respond this strongly to a man, knew how deeply you could be drawn in by the right kiss—a kiss like this.

He was tasting her, drinking her in now, with a focused sensuality that was total. His arms had wrapped around her, pulling her against him, and his mouth was relentless yet wonderful, drifting a little to the side and down to her neck, to her ear and back to claim her lips again.

They were standing in the centre of the room, and although her own height of five feet nine was slightly above average Max was a good six inches taller, making him bend to reach her and unconsciously coax her to arch upwards a little.

'Oh, Paula, you taste so sweet,' he muttered huskily, and she could hear that his breathing was already as ragged as her own. 'This feels so good…'

'Mmm…' It was a cat-like sound, fuzzy with her own need. Her arms tightened against his back, and she loved the strength of it, and the warmth, and the rippling weight of his muscles.

If she could just stay like this for hours and not *think*…

He must have felt her increasing intensity because he

responded with a groan that shuddered through his whole length, and his hands came down to bracket her hips then drift even lower to cup her behind through the soft fabric of her shorts and slip to the smooth skin of her thighs.

'You feel so fabulous,' he said. 'Every inch of you, against me like this. Your legs. Your hips. Your breasts.'

The word hit her like a fist in the face, and she almost shook her head and blurted it straight out.

Not my breasts. You don't know. Not my breasts.

It was a tribute to the realistic contour and weight of the external prosthesis she wore. He couldn't tell. There had been no stiffening or suspicion, no horrified realisation. That should, perhaps, be regarded as good news…

She couldn't think of it that way, though. She felt immediately as if she were deceiving him, and yet she was so far from being ready to *tell* him about it that she couldn't even begin to think of how she could do it, the words she would use.

Instead, she froze for one horrible moment and then began to fight him off—not violently, but in the way that a sixteen-year-old would with a boy of her own age who was trying to go too far too fast. She slid her hands down the rope of his forearms and plucked his hand from her thigh, then twisted in his arms to protect her breasts even as his other hand was about to run lightly over her right breast's gentle swell. She hunched her shoulders, turned her head aside and, in a voice that was weak and hunted, said 'N-no…'

He stilled warily, and his grey eyes narrowed. 'What is it, Paula?'

'Nothing. We just…have to stop, that's all.'

He waited, clearly expecting more, and when she only stared down in silence he probed gently, 'Why?'

She was a thousand miles from being able to tell him. It just wasn't the sort of information you shared on a first date, especially if you weren't yet sure you would agree to a second one. And if you didn't agree to the oh-so-significant second date, was that purely because you were running away? Finally, was running away merely sensible, or the behaviour of a coward?

He, in his turn, wasn't the sort of man you could fob off, however. He was searching her with his grey gaze, his frown troubled. He could tell that there was more to this than just coyness, yet she mustn't let him follow that idea too far or he would guess…

'I just…don't want to go any further, that's all. I'm…not like that, and this isn't what I want.'

'You seemed to want it a few minutes ago,' he accused silkily.

'Oh, and you were hoping to get lucky, were you?' she shot back, the words clumsy.

'No! For God's sake, Paula!' he ground out, and she knew she'd pushed him too far.

Perversely, it made her feel safe. If he was angry with her…

'That's *not* what I meant, and you know it!' he said. 'We've had a wonderful evening. Warm, interesting… I haven't felt so alive in, well, I don't know how long. We've talked, laughed together.'

'Yes,' she said, 'so why can't it stop there? Why does it have to go further? Why is there always sex for a man, like his reward for putting on a good show? As if the only point to our eating together, being together, was to lead up to bed—soften me up for it, or whatever you've been trying to do.'

'Hell, Paula!' He loomed over her, his anger intensely virile. 'I don't believe you're wording it in that way! Is that really what you think I've been playing at all evening? Are you really going to try and deny that you've been as aware of me as I've been of you? I'm *not wrong* about that! I know I'm not! I'm not that arrogant and lacking in perception!

'And I'm a grown man and you're a mature woman.

There's no power play in this. You were free to respond or not to respond at any point, just as I was. This is happening between equals, Paula, not between someone who is trying to trick or manipulate and someone who can be manipulated. Don't try and pretend now! You *wanted* this!'

'Yes, and now I want it to stop,' she returned tightly. 'That's simple enough, isn't it?'

He spread his hands, still helplessly angry, and she could hardly blame him. Anger, though, was better than the kindness she knew she would have seen in him if she'd told him the truth. Oh, yes! The idea of kindness from a man like Max Costain made her feel positively sick.

'OK,' he said abruptly. 'It's stopped.'

'Thank you.'

'And I'm going. Thanks for the coffee and cake.'

'And thanks for our picnic. It was wonderful. I—I've really had a very good time, Max.'

'Have you?' He cocked an eyebrow. 'I now doubt the whole thing. Perhaps you took me seriously and *did* practise that smile in the mirror, along with a whole lot of other things, like the way you flick the hair back from your neck, the way you cover your mouth when you think you shouldn't be laughing then press your lips against the knuckle of your forefinger and break away to toss your head.

'Maybe you've been practising the way you listen, too, and the way you eat and walk and ask me questions—just a little tentative, but with your eyes telling me how much you really want to hear the answer. Or that's what I thought, anyway. But perhaps you've been practising all that and just got too damned good at it!'

'N-no, Max… No! I meant… I *mean* everything that happened tonight. Everything I did was real. I just—'

'Changed your mind halfway through?' he offered helpfully, in a tone of spun steel.

'Yes. Yes, I did. I changed my mind.'

'And I'd be the first to insist that you had every right to do so,' he answered heavily, 'if you were seventeen. As it is, I wonder if you shouldn't know yourself and your needs and desires a little better by now.'

'OK, Max.' She closed her eyes. 'I'm sorry.'

'Believe it or not, so am I.'

He walked towards the door and she didn't try to stop him, knowing at last how right he was to have accused her. Looking back, she knew she *had* been sending signals, not consciously or deliberately but just as strongly as he'd suggested. She had felt so alive in his company, her senses singing, her humour quick, her perceptions heightened... No wonder he had seen it, no wonder he had been bemused when she'd suddenly switched it all off.

And his anger a few minutes later, when she'd done all she could to provoke it, was even easier to understand.

'Goodnight, Max,' she offered as he reached the door, and it came out so bleak and bereft that he turned and frowned again, hesitating for just a second as if wondering, suddenly, if all was not as it seemed.

Too afraid at the possibility of having him read her, she flicked her gaze down and started a feverish inspection of her cuticles. A few seconds later she heard the door quietly click behind him.

The house shrieked its emptiness now. The compact disc Max had put on was long finished and the place was silent. An hour and a half ago, if she had resisted the need to invite him in, the solitude and silence would have seemed welcoming to her and almost nourishing. Now, they were painful and unbearable.

She clattered down the two steps to her slightly sunken living room and went immediately to the television, grabbing the remote on top of it and darting her finger to the 'on' button, a nervous little gesture that brought Kelly Rainer's confident blonde presence almost instantly into the room.

Which meant that it was quite a bit later than she'd thought. After eleven, because this was the Channel Six news.

'Up next,' Kelly Rainer said, 'a new beauty pageant in Zuma—for the under fives. We'll look at those adorable pictures after these messages...'

'Oh, good grief, Kelly, is that really what passes for news at this time of night?' Paula groaned at the smile on the screen, just before it gave way to a rather nauseating commercial for an over-the-counter sleeping tablet.

She switched the television off again, preferring, after all, the silence.

CHAPTER FIVE

MAX glanced down at his appointment sheet, after returning from lunch at one-twenty on a Thursday six days after his evening with Paula at Catalina Canyon. The first entry read, '1.30 p.m. BLENCO, Elinor, 5. Last visit—ear infection, sore throat.'

He sighed, pressed the heels of his hands against his eyes, then stretched his face muscles in an attempt to focus and clear his head.

Normally, the name Blenco on his appointment sheet would have given him a feeling of pleasant anticipation. David Blenco was Zuma's mayor, and a personal friend. Widowed suddenly two years ago, he was perhaps the only person in politics, local or otherwise, whom Max both trusted and liked, and in the midst of his heavy workload he still found time and energy to do a superb job as the lone parent to his two children—five-year-old Elinor and three-year-old Daniel.

Sometimes the children were brought in by David's mother, who was very involved in their care, but more often it was David himself, and Max usually squeezed in some extra time for a talk. Today, though, he was reluctant to face a friend. He had too much on his mind, and David was likely to spot the fact. Not that he'd probe the issue openly, but there were times when talking about sport, sport and more sport was just too painfully laboured and obvious.

'Have a great time at Disneyland, Sarah!' he heard Paula say in the corridor outside, and her clear, smooth voice had its usual effect on him.

He wanted her, plain and simple. It wasn't the way

some men raged with desire for a stranger with a good figure glimpsed on the street. From the very beginning it had been more than that, and it grew daily into an increasingly complex feeling...

And he was absolutely furious with her! With himself, too.

I should run a mile, he thought. A woman of her intelligence and maturity who still doesn't know what she wants? The danger signals in that are bright red and ten feet high. I don't need a walking bundle of neuroses in my life, thanks!

And yet...

Max was a man who had been brought up to respect women—to respect, in particular, women with intelligence, courage and drive, and no one in Paula's professional position got there without those qualities. So if she did perceive a problem, looming in their relationship, perhaps it was a real one, and perhaps he shouldn't be so quick to judge.

It wasn't simply that she wasn't attracted to him. He had far too much confidence in his own perceptions and in her innate honesty to conclude that. He also knew that he wasn't a man who gave up easily. His frustration last Friday night had turned too quickly to anger, he decided.

'I'm going to push—gently, if I can manage to—but I'm not going to let this slide,' he muttered aloud, pressing his fists together. It was a gesture of decision. 'I'm not going to baulk at the first hurdle. We're *both* worth more than that!'

Rising, he went to greet David Blenco and his daughter in the examination room across the corridor, his mind considerably eased. After he'd pronounced Elinor to be fighting fit and doing beautifully in every respect, he stayed to talk to David—about city politics, thank goodness, not sport—while the nurse prepared to give the five-year-old her scheduled immunisations.

'I'm not going to cry, Daddy,' Elinor announced, with large, serious blue eyes.

'I know,' David answered, just as serious as his daughter.

Max had to hide a smile, and when the shots came a moment later Elinor was true to her word.

'4.00 p.m. HASHER, Charlotte, 16. Last visit—well check-up,' announced the line on Paula's Thursday appointment printout.

This was Sam Hasher's older sister, and it was, judging by the girl's tentative manner, the first time she had ever come to the doctor without a parent.

Paula's appointment with Sam himself wasn't until the following Monday. This appointment with his sister she saw immediately as a bonus. If there was a family problem, as she strongly suspected...

'What's brought you here today, then, Charlotte?' she asked the sixteen-year-old sympathetically.

'Well, my skin for a start.' It showed the mild acne which so many teenagers cursed, but it was superficial and by no means serious. Charlotte clearly didn't feel this way, though. 'One of my friends takes antibiotics for hers, and I'd like to take them, too,' she finished confidently.

Paula resisted her immediate temptation to express horror at the idea and dismiss it out of hand. 'Her acne must be pretty severe, then,' she said carefully.

'Oh, yes, it used to be really gross. But it's improved since she started on the antibiotics, you see, and if mine improved the same amount it'd be gone altogether.'

'Well, I don't know, Charlotte. Antibiotics are such amazing drugs that it's tempting to think they'll work for everything, with no down-side attached, but that's not true. They're not very selective, for a start, and they kill off the good organisms that your body needs as well as the bad ones.'

'Good organisms?'

'Believe it or not, there are some, and they're important! The bacteria that your digestive tract needs, for example. And you don't want the bacteria in your system to become resistant to them, either. I wouldn't prescribe antibiotics for anything but the most severe and intractable acne, and you just don't have that.'

'So you're saying I have to live with it?'

'Not at all! There's a lot you can do, one of the most important things being to remember that it will clear up in time, and if you're careful to leave it *alone*—'

'You mean, don't squeeze?'

'Very definitely—then it won't scar. There are some good over-the-counter treatments you can get to apply to your skin to cleanse it and head off a bad break-out and, yes, I know they don't always just magic the problem away, but you have to be a little patient. Your diet is important, and so is getting exercise and good sleep. I have a couple of pamphlets I'll give you, OK?'

'Sure...' Charlotte was clearly disappointed that Paula was not possessed of a magic wand.

'Now, was there anything else?' Somehow, she sensed strongly that there was.

'Well, yes, my periods,' the awkward and rather plump teenager said.

'Painful?'

'Not just painful. I...just hate them, that's all. I don't get one for six weeks then suddenly, boom! Floods! And then another one two and a half weeks later. I hate not knowing when they're going to come. I hate feeling bloated for days. I hate the pain. Isn't there anything you can do?'

She seemed genuine in her complaint, and hopeful of the existence of another magic wand, yet there was an undercurrent in her, too, as there was in her brother Sam. More was going on beneath the surface. Paula drew out a few more details about Charlotte's symptoms to satisfy herself that the story was at least convincing in theory then, watching carefully for a reaction, said, 'I could put you on the Pill...'

Some teenage girls were canny enough to complain of difficult periods as a way of getting a contraceptive prescription and, while Paula considered a protected sexually active girl to be a lot better than an equally active girl who wasn't protected, she was always cautious about the possibility of being manipulated. Sometimes she was tempted to echo a frustrated parent's complaint that dealing with ear infections and diaper rash was a picnic, compared to what followed in the teen years. This time, though...

Charlotte looked horrified. 'The Pill? Mom would die! Because if Dad found out he'd—' She stopped abruptly. 'No, is there something else? Or...or can you call it something else, if the Pill is the only thing?'

'*Call* it something else?'

'Yes. Like iron tablets, or something. Just put it in one of those regular bottles and label it iron tablets.'

'No, I really couldn't,' Paula answered gently. 'But could I talk to your father...' The suggestion sounded lame even as she made it. Her impression of Ray Hasher was that her professional role would carry little weight with him. If she tried to explain that she was prescribing a contraceptive pill for medical reasons...

This was confirmed by Charlotte's next words.

'Don't,' she begged hastily. 'Please. I'll just go on taking the pain relief stuff. It's really not that bad. And it's going to settle down eventually anyway, isn't it?'

'Most women find that it does,' Paula agreed. 'In your late teens or early twenties, or after you've had a child.'

'Mom and Dad are separating,' the girl suddenly announced, in an abrupt way, as if this was what had been simmering in her mind all along. 'They really are this time, Mom says. When that happens, I'll come back and get the Pill 'cos Mom will understand. It's just Dad.'

'Your parents have tried separating before?' Paula asked, even more alert now.

'Well, no, I mean, sort of.' Charlotte made a face. 'Mom...always talks her way out of it.'

'You mean she persuades your dad to have another try at the marriage?'

'No! It's not Dad that wants to leave. He—' Once again she stopped abruptly after the mention of her father.

'He's pretty harsh on you, isn't he?' Paula suggested gently.

'He hates us, but he won't *leave.* Oh, geez, why am I telling you this? Sam's trying to make him leave by seizing all over the place. That new stuff you've got him on—he never even takes it. Mom thinks he does, but I know. He flushes it. Dad hates Sam's seizures. I think it'd work if Mom just got the courage to kick him out.'

She stopped again and looked squarely at Paula, cunning and desperate at the same time, the deeper purpose of her visit clear now. 'You can't get him to leave, can you?'

Oh, dear, she really does have faith in me! Paula thought.

'Make up an even worse health reason? Dad hates sickness and doctors. When Sam got diagnosed with epilepsy, when he was seven, that's when it all got horrible, really. If you said I had a syndrome...I don't care what. Tell him it's degenerative, and the treatment's going to cost a fortune. Tell him I'll lose my hair. I even *would* lose my hair.'

She laughed, though shakily, and Paula suddenly saw what a bright, pretty girl she was—or had the potential to be. 'You and Sam are close, aren't you?'

'Helps.'

There was a silence. Quite a long one. Paula finally said, 'Charlotte, I really can't pretend you've got ''a syndrome''.'

'I guess not. A palindrome?' she suggested cheekily, and wryly.

'And I can't prescribe a divorce for your parents.'

'No...'

'But now that I know what's going on—and I had suspected something, actually—I can at least tell your mother how dangerous it is for Sam to be doing what he's doing.'

'*Dangerous?* Is it?'

'Yes! He seems to be able to induce the seizures deliberately...'

'I know, but don't ask me how. He won't tell me.'

'But if he's skipping medication, what if he has one accidentally...?'

'Oh, he does, sometimes.'

'Like when he's just about to start down a set of concrete stairs, like the ones outside this office.'

Charlotte looked shocked. 'That wouldn't happen.'

Oh, the confidence of teenagers in their own and each other's invincibility!

'It very easily could,' Paula insisted. 'I get the feeling you're both getting more desperate. If he cuts his medication too much and too suddenly it could lead to a fatal seizure.'

Charlotte looked appalled. 'I—I guess we both thought...that he was pretty much in control of the whole thing. But he's not, is he?'

'No, he's not, and I'm going to call your mother and have both of them come in tomorrow first thing, even though that means him cutting school. Now that you've told me what's going on, I don't want to stall any longer on this!'

So Sam's appointment was changed again, and this time Paula didn't care that she alarmed Mrs Hasher over the phone, nor that she alarmed her the next morning when she said to Sam, 'Now, do you want to tell your mother what you've been doing to precipitate your seizures, and why?'

What she'd failed to anticipate, though, was the teenager's sense of drama. Before she could anticipate what he intended, Sam had strolled to the window, calmly looked out at the bright Arizona morning sun in the eastern sky, raised his fingers and flicked them rapidly up and down in front of his eyes to create a strobe effect. Just seconds later his brain and his body obediently gave their response, and he fell to the floor, thrashing uncontrollably as contorted sounds fell from his lips.

Mrs Hasher cried out and immediately dropped to her knees and pulled a clean handkerchief from her pocket to insert between her son's teeth, while Paula slipped a rolled towel beneath his head and checked that his T-shirt was loose enough around his neck. Mrs Hasher then watched and waited for the seizure to end as Paula was doing, clearly anxious and upset about it, although she'd dealt with seizures like this many times before.

'It doesn't usually go on as long as this,' she said tensely, and Paula shared her perception that the seconds were passing very slowly.

There was a sharp knock at the door, and it opened almost before she'd called, 'Come in!' There was Max, his eyebrows raised and his face alert.

Mrs Hasher hadn't even noticed him come in. 'OK... OK... It's passing now,' she was murmuring, still intently focused on her son. 'I recognise this. It's ending.'

'Heard the noise. Everything all right?' Max said quietly.

'Remember that story you told me a couple of weeks ago about the epileptic boy in your class?' she replied in the same murmuring tone. 'Sam's been showing off, too. There's more to it than that, of course. We're starting to get to the bottom of it now.'

'You don't need me, then?'

'Thanks, but no.'

They both glanced towards Sam and his mother, then Max let himself out again, leaving Paula with her usual tangle of feelings on his account.

It was almost a week since their picnic in Catalina Canyon, and things had been distinctly tense since then. Max approached her warily. At the partners' meeting on Tuesday afternoon he had carefully sat next to Deborah, and had let Brian do the lion's share of questioning as to how she was settling in after her first two weeks in the practice.

When they met in the corridor, which they did constantly throughout the day as they shuttled between the patients, waiting for them in different examination rooms, his body language betrayed distance and prickliness, and his snatched phrases of small talk were glib, obvious and uninspiring, as if he wasn't going to waste any effort on wit or depth with her.

She could hardly blame him yet she hated it more and more, very aware of something very precious that she had just begun to discover, only to lose it again. Feeling so distant from him made her even more conscious of her attraction to him than she had been a week ago, when there'd been as yet nothing concrete to cloud it, and she actually went weak sometimes when she encountered him at a moment when she hadn't steeled herself for it.

It had happened just now, and she had to fight the feeling to concentrate on Sam, who was sitting up slowly now and saying rather groggily, 'Gee, that was a bad one, wasn't it? I'm getting a headache already...'

'Sam, you crazy kid,' his mother was saying on a moan that was half angry, half badly shaken. 'You do this *deliberately?*'

He shrugged—that same shrug which had first aroused Paula's curiosity two and a half weeks ago. 'Are you going to tell her why?' she prompted him.

'*Why,* Sam?' Mrs Hasher asked, before he could even begin to reply.

'So Dad'll leave, of course,' he muttered. Then he swore, and his voice cracked. 'Just so he'll get to the point where he'll *leave,* that's all.'

Ultimately, it really wasn't a medical problem. Paula hunted up a painkiller sample to give Sam for the increasing headache, which many epileptics suffered after a *grand mal* seizure, and told him in no uncertain terms about the danger in what he'd been doing.

He agreed that Mrs Hasher would supervise the taking of his medication more closely, and that it was his own behaviour that had earned this childish treatment.

'Now, did you take *any* of the second drug?' Paula asked him.

'A couple of doses.'

'But you skipped several doses of the usual?'

'Yes.'

'Then very possibly you can continue the regime you've been on all along, although we're going to follow all that very carefully.'

That dealt with the purely physiological aspect of the problem. The Hasher family still needed help, though.

In that area, all Paula could do was to pass on a few pamphlets about support services, and when Sam had gone to the bathroom, still feeling rather washed out and sleepy following the strong seizure, she urged Mrs Hasher, 'Both your children seem very keen for your marriage to end, and that's a little unusual. Often kids want their parents to stay together way beyond the point where a reconciliation is realistic. It suggests that they're really hurting over your husband's behaviour, to the point where Sam was prepared to—'

'Yes,' Mrs Hasher interrupted. 'It's...it's been a shock. I must start to make the move to leave. No,' she corrected herself firmly at once, 'I must just *leave.* I don't think the kids have realised that—that we'll have to be the ones to leave our home. It'll be hard, financially, because I know he won't pay support, but it's the only way.'

There was bleakness, coupled with resolve, in her face.

All this made a difficult start to the day, and by lunchtime Paula felt she must have borrowed Sam's post-ictal headache and had to down two pills in order to get through the afternoon. In that, she was considerably helped by several well-baby checks on happy, healthy infants and told each mother sincerely, 'He's beautiful!' or 'She's doing really well!'

She thought the day had been completely salvaged by five o'clock, and even though it was her first turn to take weekend call she didn't expect it to be too onerous. There was physician's assistant Mary Gibbons to respond to the more routine phone questions during daytime hours, and any true emergency was referred immediately to the hospital, which left only what fell in between, as well as the hospital rounds that she would make on Saturday and Sunday mornings.

But then she met Max again in the corridor, and as usual found it difficult to disguise her mixed-up, reluctant and physically dizzying feelings for him. This time he noticed—he was observing her quite intently—and stopped her with a hand hard on her forearm to say in a low, demanding tone, 'Are you afraid of me, Paula? Or what? What *is* it with you? I'd swear...'

His forefinger began to caress her arm gently, hypnotising and locking her gaze, and she knew it was a deliberate attempt to draw out her response. Would she flinch and pull away? Politely disentangle herself from the oddly private moment that had overtaken them both in the midst of a still-busy practice? No...

'Max...'

'Look!' he said softly. 'Look what's happening! You're drifting closer. These little hairs...they're almost too fine to be called hairs...are standing on end. If I took your pulse now...' He twisted his hand so that his thumb was resting across her wrist. 'Yes, it's starting to race. I've been so angry with you, Paula, for making a fool of me...'

'I didn't. I wasn't,' she insisted, low and urgent. 'Not that, Max. It was all in me, not you.'

'Then *tell* me.'

And the connection between them was so strong and his effect on her so powerful and draining that all she could do was blurt the truth. 'I—I just need time, that's all, to work out if I *can*—'

'Time?' he echoed the word. 'Is it—? Well, I know you're divorced. Brian mentioned it.'

'Yes.'

She'd meant, yes, she was divorced, but he'd taken it further to mean, yes, she needed time because of the divorce and said quickly, his voice a little husky, 'Then, of course! A divorce is...can be...a big thing. People do need time. God, Paula, why didn't you say so before?'

'Max, no. Hang on a minute! My divorce was—'

Brian came churning down the corridor at that moment, mouthing some medical gobbledygook that didn't make any sense at all to Paula for several seconds until she realised he was talking to her, telling her in more detail about a newborn he'd mentioned to her earlier in the day who wasn't looking quite right and needed her special attention tomorrow during her hospital round.

With difficulty, she wrenched her focus around to where it needed to be and asked a couple of questions, to be given the vague reply, 'Maybe it's nothing. The indications were very slight. Low birthweight—only five pounds at term. And with some hypotonia. The parents heard a nurse use that word and wanted to know what it meant. Now they're a bit alarmed. Poor muscle tone. I mean, I wish we could tell them. Maybe it really is nothing.'

'That's not very satisfactory, Brian,' Max pointed out on a drawl, his sharp mind immediately drawn into the problem.

'I know,' he agreed. 'It's not. But, hey, this is pediatrics, not mechanical engineering.'

'What's your best guess, then, Brian?' Paula begged.

'Mosaic Down's syndrome? There are most of the facial signs, but they're not very clear-cut. Those could just be…what the little girl looks like.' He spread his hands. 'That's why I want a second opinion before the parents are told anything. I'm angry at that nurse! I'll give *her* hypotonia! She should have been more careful.'

'OK, well, I'll take a really good look tomorrow,' Paula promised, and Brian strode on, calling for Susan Clifford, the office manager, with an impatience that managed to be both peremptory and cheerful at the same time.

'Brian has impeccable timing on occasion,' Max muttered. 'I guess this is a hopeless place for any kind of a talk.'

This last was added as Kathy, one of the nursing assistants, came past to unload fresh supplies in the drawers and cupboards of the little kitchen alcove where they stood.

'Cheer up, Dr Costain, renovations should be finished in two weeks,' she said, making a plausible interpretation of his sour look, as a loud drill began to whine and hiccup and whine again at the far end of the corridor.

'Hopeless,' Paula murmured in agreement to Max.

'No, really, I think they will,' Kathy insisted brightly, and when she'd passed on a few seconds later both Max and Paula laughed. Paula gave up, too, on the possibility of clarifying the issue of her divorce at this moment—that it had been amicable, that it was long over, that she needed time for other reasons. It would have to wait.

And she was guiltily conscious within herself that she was happy, rather than otherwise, about his misinterpretation...until a thought struck her. What good is it going to do me to buy time? No amount of time will bring my body back the way it once was. I must decide...how much I'm brave enough to risk with Max, whether I want to go on with this...whether I *can,* and then, as soon as we have some time together, tell him the truth.

Like taking home a briefcase full of work to do on the weekend, Paula took the issue home with her, determined that by Monday morning she would have thought the whole thing through. She envisaged it as a lengthy and difficult grappling with the whole gamut of her feelings, from her growing attraction to Max on the one hand to her very real fears of rejection on the other, until an understanding of her future course was won by sheer force of effort but, in fact, as it turned out, the moment of decision was nothing like that...

'Paula?'

It was Max's voice, waking her at half past eleven that same night, not long after she had fallen asleep.

'Yes? What...?' Alertness was slow to return.

'Are you ready to come and assist with some quads?'

'Oh, she's in labour?' Now she was wide awake.

'Yes, it's strong and not stopping this time. I got a call from Ben Liddell, the chief of Neonatology, a few minutes ago. They're prepping her already so get your skates on.'

Paula hunted up one of her well-worn green scrub suits and put it on, and was out of the house within five minutes of Max's call. They arrived at the hospital together—the sight of him clad only in the fine, soft fabric of his scrubs made her strength dissolve into the floor in seconds—and went straight up to the maternity floor, gave their hands and arms a thorough washing and put on shoe covers, gowns, caps and masks. The babies would be born by Caesarean section, with Mrs Carey under epidural anaesthesia so that she was fully conscious at the birth.

Looking through the big window that opened between the corridor and the obstetric OR, Paula saw that the process of prepping the patient was already well under way. She was draped and had the tube which delivered her anaesthesia snaking up out of the back of her gown. She was strapped to the table, connected to a drip and a catheter and appeared almost swamped by all this gear—and by the crowd of people already gathered around her.

Mr Carey, seated beside his wife, looked strained and frightened, his lips a tight line below his dark moustache. In the corridor four preemie warming beds with attached ventilators stood waiting, labelled 'Quad 1', 'Quad 2', 'Quad 3' and 'Quad 4'.

'Here's Ben and his team,' Max said, and another surge of medical personnel approached, all dressed in scrubs and all immediately reaching for masks, caps and gowns.

With teams of four responsible for each quad, Lisa Carey would deliver her babies in the presence of well over twenty people.

'She's almost thirty-three weeks,' Max commented to Paula as they entered. 'Hopefully we're overdoing it here. Ben says her sonogram two days ago showed that at least three of the babies were a good size for their gestational age—'

'OK, people,' announced the obstetrician, Jeffrey Allan.

Nurses were wheeling in the four 'ambulettes'—special, open cribs, warmed from above, which could be moved easily between here and the N.I.C.U. on the floor above. The anaesthesiologist confirmed that Lisa was numb, and the obstetrician began his work, using an incision down the middle of her abdomen instead of the less invasive low transverse incision in order to facilitate the quick, safe removal of each baby.

The entire delivery took only minutes, but Paula was aware of little of it, as she had been assigned to the team dealing with quad 1. The girl—'Georgia,' said Lisa at once—would have looked tiny to most people, but in fact for a quad born at less than thirty-three weeks gestation she was wonderfully sturdy.

'Over four pounds, I'd say,' Paula guessed aloud as she suctioned out fluid and mucus from the baby's nose and throat.

The N.I.C.U. nurses and pediatric resident assisting her both nodded.

Georgia lay limp for just a few seconds, then a few gentle flicks from Nurse Monica Seaman brought strong breathing and the first cry.

Lisa gave an exclamation of delight at the sound and her husband was so emotional that a nurse, assisting with the delivery, had to coax him quite firmly back into his seat.

The cry was definitely good news, but no one relaxed yet. Paula and the resident, Troy Wheeler, attached a heart monitor and pulse oxymeter, while Nurse Seaman covered the tiny head in a little knitted cap to help retain body heat, then successfully inserted a drip into the tiny arm to replenish the fluid loss that occurred rapidly through fine skin which as yet had only the thinnest layer of fat beneath.

In the background, meanwhile, the second quad was born. She was another girl, Hayley, and was significantly smaller, Paula gathered from the exchanges between members of Hayley's team. Still, though, her delivery had been quick and uncomplicated, and she was breathing on a ventilator within a few minutes.

Now things started to slow down ominously. This next quad would be Max's, but the wait seemed long as the baby's position was not good—high up under Mrs Carey's ribs, and with one more baby tangled there, too.

'OK, let's go,' Paula heard herself say firmly, and

Georgia's first journey outside the womb commenced, along the corridor and up in the elevator to the N.I.C.U. at the far end of the next floor. It was like closing a book at the height of the plot's climax, but she had no choice. They'd done everything they needed to do for Georgia here, and they needed to get her upstairs to the unit.

'Downward pressure *now,* Lindsay,' Paula heard Jeffrey Allan say to his nurse just as the operating room door closed behind her.

It was another fifteen minutes before Max's baby, the only boy, arrived in the N.I.C.U., all three of his sisters having arrived ahead of him. Although the last girl to be born, Audrey weighed over three pounds and had managed some weak breaths on her own, before being placed on the ventilator.

Still absorbed in attaching more leads to monitor pulse, temperature and respiratory rate, as well as taking the first of what in some preemies could be an endless series of blood tests, Paula could only look up briefly when Max arrived at last and had his ambulette wheeled next to hers.

'Say hi to your sister, Alex,' Max said softly, and then he was at work again.

It was an hour and a half before he finally ceded responsibility for the tiny boy to Ben Liddell and his team. Paula, too, was free to go now. In fact, she could have left half an hour earlier, but there was something about Max which had held her here, talking to the staff about the three baby girls while she remained at all times vitally aware of Max and his movements.

There was something so focused about him, heroic yet deeply compassionate. He wasn't the type who'd have bullied a tiny baby like this into survival. Without yet fully acknowledging what it meant, she knew that his advent in her life was something precious, something that it would hurt very much to lose.

They left the unit together, at last able to remove the paraphernalia of caps and masks.

'Ben's asked us to see the Careys on our way out,' he said, 'though Ben himself will be down with them a little later, once Lisa is in her own room.'

'What's your sense of the babies, Max?' Paula asked, her instinct being to trust his judgement even more than her own.

'Well, your Georgia looks great. She has every chance of going home with her mother in the middle of next week as long as she's started to gain and feed well. And the other two girls looked good, too.'

'Alex, though…'

'Alex,' Max agreed. 'And yet…there was a very clear moment back there when he chose to live, Paula. We had to resuscitate him. His heart had stopped, and we bagged him with oxygen by hand before we tried to get a tube into his lungs. And in that moment, between the bag and the tube… You know that moment. Excruciating…'

'Yes, it can seem endless, trying to get a tube down a baby that small.'

'He breathed by himself twice. It was a struggle. He couldn't have kept it up, but—tell me I'm romanticising, if you like—it really felt like he'd signalled his will to fight. He was moving quite vigorously, too. He'd *chosen* to fight. He'd chosen life.'

Click! Something in Paula responded profoundly to Max's simple phrase. She didn't have time to analyse the feeling just now, though. They were at the stairs and on their way down to the recovery suite adjacent to the obstetric OR.

Mrs Carey and her husband, Curtis, were there, Mrs Carey still under frequent monitoring, catheterised and receiving intravenous fluids. With the severe stretching of her uterus caused by carrying four placentas and over twelve pounds of baby, post-partum haemorrhage was a danger to be alert for, and her incision, too, was unusually large. She would be watched very carefully over the next few days before discharge.

Both new parents were too tired and overcome by the experience of the birth to react strongly to Max's careful summary of the condition of the babies, and didn't have any questions, so the visit didn't take very long.

Paula's bed began to beckon more strongly by the minute, and when, on the steps outside the main lobby of the hospital, she was suddenly dazzled by bright lights she was for a long moment quite disoriented.

What was *this?*

It was a television camera crew, and Kelly Rainer swooping at them, microphone in hand. It must be an important story if she'd been sent to cover it so late at night. The cameras were evidently rolling, too, because she was speaking in her best journalese.

'But amidst the tragedy of tonight's nightclub fire, with the confirmed deaths of two people and over thirty more seriously injured, comes the news of a far happier event, the birth of Zuma's first set of quads. Dr Max Costain, how are the babies, and how are their parents?'

Max narrowed his eyes and frowned at the camera while Paula was still taking in the news that there had been another drama at the hospital tonight.

'I'm not authorised to say anything at all at this stage, Kelly,' he said, 'so I'm sorry I won't be able to answer any questions right now.'

'But the babies have been born, isn't that right?' she persisted. 'They're all living?'

'I'm sorry, I can't comment at this stage.'

'OK, cut,' Kelly Rainer called to her cameraman, clearly annoyed.

'That wasn't live?' Max asked.

'No, delayed feed, but damn it, Max, you've got to say *something!*'

'Stick to your main story,' he said. 'I had no idea you were going to be here, Kelly.'

'Neither did I...I mean, for the quads...but it counterpoints the fire story so beautifully. Please, Max, couldn't you—?'

'No,' he answered firmly, then, in a much lower tone as he bent towards Paula, 'Head back inside and go out through the south wing. I can handle this, and you don't need to get caught up in it.' The brief feathering of his touch on her bare arm left fire, although it was gone again in a moment.

A second media crew from a rival television station had closed in now, obviously aware that there was something they were missing, so Paula didn't argue and slipped back inside as Kelly Rainer had her camera and sound turned on again and began another on-camera attempt at getting something out of Max. The two had obviously encountered each other somewhere before, with the accompaniment of sparks...

It was well after two o'clock by the time Paula crawled wearily into bed, not knowing whether Max had been talked into an interview about the quads or not. Somehow, her money was on not. She was beginning to have the strong suspicion that Max generally got what he wanted. In relation to herself and their fragile new relationship, for example...

She knew that, without any conscious effort and emotional wrestling at all, her decision was now made. Choosing life. Max had used the words about baby Alex tonight.

'And I choose life, too,' Paula said aloud to the darkened room. It was a heartfelt vow. 'I choose to trust Max, and I choose to find the courage to go on with this.'

It didn't mean she wouldn't be scared, but to give in to that fear... 'I won't! I *will* believe in my own future and that a man like Max could care...'

CHAPTER SIX

AGAINST the ongoing backdrop of the dramatic nightclub fire, the rest of Paula's weekend passed, with her medical duties relatively light. As a doctor, she didn't have anything to do with the tragedy, but watched the flame-filled footage on the news, heard Kelly Rainer's generally responsible coverage and shared Zuma's elation and sadness as most of the casualties were pronounced out of danger, while three more lost their lives.

In her own professional role, she saw the baby girl that Brian had been concerned about and agreed with his perception that the child 'wasn't looking quite right'. There were several of the physical signs that indicated Down's syndrome—a flattened bridge of the nose, greyish-white spots like grains of salt around the edges of each iris and an unusually large, protruding tongue—and yet the signs weren't nearly as marked as she had seen in other babies.

Brian had called in a heart specialist on Friday, who had found no suggestion of the heart defects from which approximately thirty-five per cent of Down's syndrome children suffered. The baby's actual state of health was good, too. There was nothing to suggest that she shouldn't be discharged that afternoon on schedule so Paula simply ordered the tests that would clarify the issue and made a note to discuss with Brian on Monday what the parents should be told.

Later on Saturday, after a refreshing nap, there was plenty of time to go through the information sheet on her pottery class, which was starting this coming Monday, and to phone the zoo and ask about volunteering there, all of which made her feel good about the fact that she was organising her life here.

She arrived at the practice on Monday morning possessed of a quiet sense of confidence.

I can do this. I can do my best to make things work—with Max, and with everything else. I don't just have to sit back and let life happen to me.

When Max teased her a little during a brief partners' meeting first thing in the morning she teased him back, and he seemed content to leave it at that, which had her thinking gratefully, He's going to let me take it at my own pace. That's already better than I dared to hope for.

There was a very definite sense, though, that he was just biding his time, that there was something special between them already and he wasn't going to let her deny that. It was there in the way he touched her whenever they passed in the corridor and in the tone he had begun to use when they exchanged a quick word between patients. He was caressing her with his voice, caressing her name every time it crossed his lips…

The other practice partners, as well as the more involved members of the ancillary staff, were beginning to suspect that something was going on, she realised. Deborah Weir caught the two of them in conversation between patients and commented to Paula later, when they were alone at the coffee-station, with a knowing nuance colouring her usually down-to-earth speech, 'Nice to see Max working so hard to help you settle in here.'

Brian, ambushing her out of the blue after a very professional discussion of Catherine Lonsdale, his new patient with the ambiguous indicators of Down's syndrome, was more direct. 'If what I think is happening is, in fact, happening, Paula, then go for it! Max is a great guy, and you two would be perfect together.'

And it was that word 'perfect' that made Paula realise that her decision over the weekend meant nothing unless she acted on it as soon as possible, no matter how much time Max himself was willing to give.

He can't go on thinking it's my divorce that's the problem, she thought. Hedging like that, at the very beginning of a relationship, doesn't exactly get it off on a good footing.

Max was divorced, too, of course, and she began to wonder what had gone wrong in his marriage. Deflecting the subject rather abruptly from Deborah's medical talk during a quick sandwich lunch at a nearby café that same day, she asked the other doctor, 'Max's marriage...had you joined the practice when it ended?'

'I joined it before it began!' Deborah retorted.

'Really? But I thought you'd only been here—'

'It didn't last very long. Three years, and they were divorced about a year ago.'

'Fairly recently.' Perhaps this was why he didn't mention it. It was too fresh and raw for him, as she'd let him believe her divorce was for her. 'Then it obviously wasn't one of those early relationships that get killed by medical school,' she went on.

'Oh, he had one of those, too,' Deborah said. 'They teetered on the edge of an engagement for a couple of years, then she winged off to some fairly intense position at the Mayo Clinic. She was very bright, apparently.'

'So is Max,' Paula retorted, too quickly.

Deborah grinned soothingly. 'Did I say he wasn't? But there's a lot more to him than brains. He has heart, too, and by all accounts Stephanie didn't. He plunged fairly deeply into his career after that...you know, those really gruelling years...then kind of catapulted out again and got married on the rebound, which rarely works.'

'No...'

'How about you?' Deborah asked. 'You've got a notch on your belt too, haven't you?'

'Yes, but mine was finished seven years ago,' she clarified absently, still thinking about Max, 'and it was quite amicable. It's history as far as my current existence goes.'

'Still, that makes three of us,' was Deborah's wry conclusion. 'Thank goodness for Brian and Wanda and their loyal spouses. And, by the way, if you know any single, heterosexual men, non-smokers, who are into mountain-biking, short women and jazz, *do* arrange an introduction because I didn't become a pediatrician just so I could look after *other* people's kids!'

'I will,' Paula promised, a little guilty because matchmaking for Deborah was not exactly uppermost in her mind at the moment. She wondered about those two women in Max's life…

That afternoon Callie Herbert came in again, with baby Thomas in her arms and fatigue and anxiety in her face. 'I'm terrified it's R.S.V.,' she said, holding the ten-day-old baby tenderly on the cotton sheeting that covered the examining table in Room Three.

'Respiratory syncytial virus?' Paula clarified, surprised. Most non-medical people, even informed mothers like Mrs Herbert, wouldn't have heard of it. 'What makes you think it might be that?'

She stepped up to the infant and Callie Herbert took her hands away. 'Well, he's feverish and congested. Elizabeth has had a cold. At least, I assumed it was a cold, but it could easily have been R.S.V., couldn't it? Because older children don't get that sick from it, but I know small babies can die. He's still so new…'

'Let's have a good look at him, then,' Paula soothed.

Instinctively, she felt that it wasn't R.S.V. Typically, that was a virus that flared in late autumn and winter in the colder parts of the country. Here in Arizona, in April, it would be unusual. Mrs Herbert was right, though, in that the disease could be fatal in infants if it wasn't treated in time, and a baby that did recover from it was then much more likely to develop asthma or other respiratory ailments later in childhood.

'My brother's newborn had it last December,' Callie was saying, confirming Paula's suspicion that she must have some personal knowledge of the disease. 'Over Christmas, it was, in Chicago, and if they hadn't got him to the hospital he really might have died, they were told. As it was, he was in Intensive Care for several days. It was very frightening, coming out of nowhere when they just thought he had a cold.'

She shuddered and frowned, biting her lip. 'Dr Nichols, please… I know I don't need to say this, but I can't help it! Please check him extra carefully, won't you? You must know how fragile life can seem after you've come through cancer. I love him so much…' Her voice cracked a little and she couldn't go on.

Paula gave her a pat of reassurance, moved by Callie's very personal appeal, put her stethoscope to her ears and listened carefully to the baby's chest. She had seen at a glance that the little boy was congested, and could feel the fever when she touched his skin. Not frighteningly high, though, if her hands were as accurate in gauging temperature as they usually were.

And his lungs were clear. The congestion was all higher up, in sinuses, nasal passages and upper chest. To make absolutely sure, she listened again, front and back, then checked heart rate, throat, ears and eyes.

'It's fine, Callie,' she was able to tell the relieved mother. 'He's not a happy camper, to be sure. What was his temperature last time you took it?'

'A hundred and one degrees.'

'With R.S.V. I would have expected it to be a little higher. No, this is just a bad cold, which often gives babies a fever in the first couple of days. Keep a close eye on him, and if that fever gets higher or if he seems worse bring him back. Phone, too, if you're in any doubt.'

'I guess I give him something for the fever…'

'You know, that's your choice,' Paula said. 'We don't

tell people to keep fever down at all costs these days because there's some evidence that allowing a certain amount of fever actually shortens the duration of the illness. I've also heard mothers of active toddlers tell me that they *have* to let their kids stay feverish or they forget they're sick and start running around all over the place, which, of course, doesn't do them much good! This little guy, though, would probably appreciate something to help him feel better.

'Meanwhile, is there anything else that you're concerned about? You were doing fine with his feeds when I saw you in hospital.'

'Still fine,' Callie said, much happier now. 'It has been a bit tough, doing it all on one side. I got so sore and felt so lopsided. I just *cried* a couple of days last week. But when I remembered how lucky I was even to have one breast, even to be *alive* and to have this gorgeous boy…'

She got a little teary again, and apologised with a watery smile. 'Sorry! Still post-partum. I had a check-up last week at the oncologist, by the way. Still cancer-free!'

'That's great, Callie!' On an impulse, she hugged the other woman briefly, felt soft arms come around her in response and—perhaps those post-partum hormones were contagious—felt her own eyes getting a little damp.

'I'll see him in a week for his next check,' she managed, and left the room so that Callie could get baby Thomas dressed again in his natty little stretch sailor-suit.

Max was on his way to his next patient, intersecting with her outside Room Four. She was quite unsurprised when he noticed her emotion and asked her quickly, 'Problem?'

'No. *Not* a problem, which is always nice.'

'It is,' he agreed, as if he was waiting for more.

'Callie Herbert's baby *doesn't* have R.S.V., and she's such a great person and a great mother...'

'Well, I haven't really met her, but I know the world needs more of them...'

'It does.' She gulped, still oddly moved. Perhaps because of all that she felt she shared with Callie...or was it all that she *didn't* share? A husband, a healthy daughter, and now a beautiful baby...

Max had hesitated for a moment and now was saying quietly, 'You sure you're OK, Paula?'

'Stop asking me that! You'll make me worse,' she laughed, whisking a tissue across her eyes.

'So you're not OK?'

'I will be,' she answered firmly, wanting to cut to the heart of things, 'when we've talked.'

'Tonight? Oops, no, I remember. Pottery, right?'

'Pottery,' she acknowledged with a smile.

'And I've got dinner at my sister's tomorrow. Come for a swim at my place after work on Wednesday?'

'It sounds perfect.'

'Good.' He brushed one finger briefly against her cheek.

She flashed her best and brightest smile. 'Well, I know I've got someone waiting in Room Five, so...'

Turning quickly, she didn't see the way he frowned after her, nor did she see Deborah emerge from her office and catch his focused scrutiny.

'Not *another* fight, you two?' Deborah drawled teasingly.

'Fighting would be preferable, actually,' was Max's terse reply. 'Tell me, Deb, help me out, here. What has Paula said to you about her divorce?'

The pottery class was relaxing and fun. Paula and her nine classmates, rank beginners all of them, were itching to use those very professional-looking potters' wheels lined up all along one wall of the spacious studio at the

Zuma College of Art and Design. For the first half of the class, though, they were kept strictly to coil pots, like children who might break the machines or themselves if they were let loose.

When teacher Anita Hinde announced that the time had come, there was much hilarity, and a large dose of frustration as well, in the process of beginning to come to grips with the new technique.

'Coming to grips being, on occasion, too *much* the right phrase,' Paula commented to the woman at the neighbouring wheel, after snagging her nearly completed pot somehow and having the grey clay shape suddenly distort and sag like a drunken man. 'How did I do that? Pinching too hard, I guess.'

She began again, and this time triumphantly completed a neat, almost symmetrical and somehow horribly ugly thing which she chose to call a vase.

'I think when it's glazed it'll come up real nice,' her neighbour told her kindly.

'Maybe I'll make a hole in the bottom of it and plant a cactus,' Paula decided, then got a second piece of clay and made another one to match—almost.

Driving home at half past nine, unrepentantly pleased with her dubious creative achievements, she had a satisfying awareness that there was clay all over her unbleached cotton T-shirt and pink chinos and a fatigue in her hands that didn't come from holding a stethoscope or a tongue depressor.

Not consciously registering the car parked directly across the street, she drove her own vehicle into the garage, using the automatic opener, then went through the connecting door into the house. She hadn't even had time to explore the likely possibility that there was clay spattered on her face when the mission bell by her front door jangled loudly.

Max.

She saw his familiar face and shoulders, distorted by

the peephole in her front door, and opened it to him quickly, her heart beginning to beat faster already. Showing up like this on her front doorstep, without warning? At this hour?

She knew he was aware of what time her pottery class finished. He must have been waiting for her. Only now did she realise that his had been the car parked opposite.

He didn't even bother with a greeting, just lunged inside, his body outwardly lazy, inwardly coiled, and said immediately, 'Just what kind of a line were feeding me last week about needing to get over your divorce, Paula? Deborah says you've been divorced for seven years! How long is it going to take you? A lifetime? I don't buy it any more, OK? You said you wanted to talk. So talk! What's really going on?'

She had started shaking before he even finished, and had to ball her fists and lift her shoulders, freezing them stiffly, to stop him from seeing. But he *did* see, of course. From the beginning of their acquaintance, he had cut right through any attempt on her part to disguise what was really going on inside her and now, confronting his urgent need and right to know the truth, she wasn't sure whether to feel terrified of this perception of his or safe because of it.

No point in considering the question, really. She remembered her brief flirtation a few weeks ago with the idea of taking up parachuting as a hobby and thought, This is it! Emotional parachuting. This is the moment where I just have to take a deep breath and jump out of that plane.

'You'd better come in, Max,' she said, more calmly than she felt.

'I *am* in,' he said.

'*Inner,* then,' she corrected. 'I mean, do you want coffee or something?'

'No, I do *not* want coffee!' he exploded. 'Don't try to deflect this, Paula!'

'I'm not. I've said I wanted to talk. I'm just trying to—'

'Buy yourself more time?' he suggested ominously. 'So you can think up some other excuse?'

'No! Is that what you think—?'

'I don't know or care what I *think* any more. I just want the truth. Something I can get my teeth into. I'm not a quitter, Paula, and yet—' He broke off, then demanded, 'Tell me! You're not...? God, I can't even think! Married? Pregnant by some other man? What's worse than that?'

'OK. OK.' She put up her hands, hating the fact that he was angry. She knew it was her own fault.

It had been clear to both of them for some days that this was very rapidly becoming more than just experimental dating, and that they both hoped it might get serious. What was more, he was a doctor and a professional colleague. If she could have found the courage to tell him ten days ago, after he'd taken her to Catalina Canyon... But it was so hard!

Her hands were still shaking, drawing attention to just how churned up she was over this, and suddenly she saw the flash of his anger flicker as he lunged towards her and pulled her imperiously against him.

'Look, you're frightening me, OK?' His eyes blazed. 'I'm afraid there really may be something to stop what's started to happen between us.'

His mouth grazed hers, a brief, searing reminder of what could flare between them if she let it, but she didn't want him touching her while she said it, didn't want to risk the physical affront of feeling him stiffen and pull away, so she splayed her fingers and pressed them against his strong chest, shaking her head and closing her eyes.

'No, Max. Just let me say it. Don't touch me.'

'All right...'

And when it finally came down to it, jumping out of the plane could only be very simple.

Folding her arms protectively across her chest, not even thinking about the betraying symbolism of the gesture, she told him. 'I had breast cancer five and a half years ago, with some lymph node involvement, for which the best form of treatment was a left side modified radical mastectomy, followed by chemotherapy. I decided against reconstruction.

'I have no breast, Max. I have to guard against anything that might bring on left-arm swelling...lymph oedema,' she amended, remembering that he'd know the medical term. 'Such as heavy lifting. I have to watch very carefully for infection in my left arm. I have a pretty major scar, and no breast tissue, and no nipple.'

'And—?' he demanded, his voice husky and rough.

'And that's why, that's why—'

'You mean, that's it? That's all?'

'That's...quite a bit, isn't it?'

'Yes... Yes!' he agreed, pushing this point aside. 'But beyond that... You're not about to tell me that the cancer has recurred and spread?'

'No. I've been cancer-free for five years.'

She heard the tight rush of his escaping breath.

'Then what this is about,' he clarified slowly, taking her shoulders and holding them with curved palms, 'what this is purely about is that you don't believe I could still want you without a breast, isn't it? That's... I want to tell you it's crazy!'

'It's not crazy,' she answered. 'It's terrifying.'

'I know. And yet I *do* want you, Paula.'

'You can't possibly tell me it's not a shock,' she accused bluntly. 'You can't possibly tell me it makes *no* difference!'

'No?' he challenged, his eyes alight with a dangerous fire. 'Just watch me, Paula. Read my lips! *It makes no difference!*'

'Don't!' She shook her head, turning away as if from a blow, then faced him again and lifted her chin with newly gathered pride. 'Don't make it worse for me...' her voice shook a little '...by saying something that's so rosy it's totally unrealistic and makes me doubt that you care for me at all. Be honest! Give me that, at least!'

'What do you mean, "at least"?' he rasped hotly. 'Do you really think I'm going to call a halt to what's been happening between us lately because of this?' He shook his head, and his eyes burned.

'A lot of men would.'

'I'm not "a lot of men", Paula. Hell, that's an insult if ever there was one! If you're asking me if I'd *prefer* that you had both breasts, the answer, of course, is yes. Otherwise it's like saying, "Gee, I'm really glad you had cancer, Paula!" No one says that. No one feels it! But does it make a difference to what I'm hoping will go on happening between us? No! Does it extinguish the desire that's been coursing inside me since about, oh, ten minutes after we met? No! And if there's only one way to prove it to you...'

He paused and watched her for a moment, and again her hands folded instinctively across her chest. She hadn't responded to his touch on her shoulders—had just accepted it, not trusting it, willing it simply to go away—yet somehow his hands were still there, and much gentler now.

'There *is* only one way, isn't there?' he added softly.

She didn't even realise what he intended at first. He took the final small pace that was needed to bring them together length to length and then his mouth swooped down and covered hers, the raw passion of it an imperious demand for her response.

A little sound tightened in her throat and her lips seemed to part of their own accord, the touch and taste of him setting her pulses on fire at once. Her hands were still held protectively, wrapped around her torso, and he didn't try to move them, just enclosed them along with the rest of her so that she was fully imprisoned in his embrace.

In any other circumstances it might have been stifling. Now, with Max, it was utterly right to be supported, held enclosed like this, and yet with that achingly vulnerable flatness on her chest still protected from his touch.

Their kiss seemed to last endlessly, and he deepened it so gradually that she felt no confronting impatience from him. She wasn't even aware of the moment when her shielding arms finally loosened and dropped to her sides, then rose to hold him, feel him, explore him, rake across his rippling, masculine back.

They hadn't spoken for a long time, but now he did, murmuring as his lips travelled from her mouth to her ear, 'How is this, Paula? How does it feel? It feels right, doesn't it? So very right...'

'Yes...'

'Then can we take it further? Please don't say no out of fear!'

'I—'

'Say no if you want to, but *not* out of fear!'

'I don't want to say no.' The words came out scratchily, and weren't easy to say. 'I'm saying yes, but there *is* fear, Max.'

'Perhaps the fear won't go until afterwards,' he suggested, and she nodded wordlessly, her throat tight, then buried her forehead against his shoulder.

'Then let's just acknowledge that, and go forward.'

'Mmm.' She still couldn't speak.

'Where is your bedroom, darling?'

Mutely she led him there, then they stood in the blackness beside the silent, neatly made bed while she heard only the pounding of blood in her own ears. The only light was what trespassed along the corridor from the wall-lamp by the front door.

'Darkness?' he asked, and in that one word was contained a dozen questions about how she felt about this, her body, the thought of him coming to know it.

'Darkness,' she echoed, firm and tremulous at the same time. 'Please!'

He didn't say anything to this, just kissed her quickly, claiming her lips, her eyebrows, her forehead, temples, hair. Then all at once he laughed. 'What is this wonderful perfume you're wearing? Eau de clay?'

'Oh...' She laughed, too. The sound was rusty. It was the last thing she'd expected to be doing just before going to bed with him. Laughing? It was wonderful! 'I was really a master craftsman on that potter's wheel! I got it everywhere. People were ducking.'

'You mean you got your hands on a pottery wheel in your first class?'

'Yep!'

'Well, I'm no expert but I'd suggest you used too much water!'

'I had to!' Her defence was indignant and spirited. 'To get the wretched thing to be something more than a blob!'

'Which it now is, I trust?'

'You'll get it for your birthday if you're not careful,' she threatened.

'Let's see now...are there any spots I've missed?' he mused, and she felt the teasing tip of his tongue on her neck just below her ear and then in the sensitive hollow above her collar-bone.

Then, before she had any idea that he was about to do so, he touched her breast. No, *not* her breast, but the moulded prosthesis that conformed to her shape but was discarded each night when she slept, along with her clothing.

Before he could work it out for himself she told him quickly, 'It's a prosthesis.' Then she added, forgetting she'd already said it a few minutes earlier, 'I—I didn't have reconstructive surgery.'

'It feels very natural,' was his quiet comment. His touch was matter-of-fact, yet achingly tender.

'To you,' she said shakily.

'To me,' he conceded. 'You haven't given me the chance to feel *you* yet. Your skin. May I take this off?'

He was sliding her baggy, clay-stained T-shirt upwards, and she had to fight to hold herself from pushing him away. He must have felt this but he didn't say anything, just continued the careful upward peeling-off until she was forced to raise her arms above her head.

Five years ago she couldn't have done that. She'd been physically unable to lift her left arm this high. It had taken months to regain full strength in her muscles, and months more before she learned how to guard against the fluid retention caused by the removal of several lymph nodes in her arm.

He had the shirt over her head now so that all that was left was her bra, with its special pocket on the left side.

'Max—!' she hissed, panicking. He'd been about to reach around and unfasten it himself, but that was too terrifying. She couldn't ask that of him, or of herself. Not yet.

Fending his hands away, she undid the catch herself and let the garment slide to the floor, then stood there, her heart pounding and her breathing shallow, intensely thankful for the concealing cloak of inky darkness now that the door was closed.

What was he thinking? Was he too confronted and afraid to touch at the final, crucial moment? As her eyes grew better accustomed to the dimness, and her breathing slowed a little to allow sound to penetrate her mind, she saw and heard that he was moving. His fingers met in the middle of his chest, then pulled outwards. Something dropped to the floor with a light sound.

He was undressing.

Feeling shaky again, she followed suit to remove her

chino pants, underwear and sandals, and then stood there breathless, waiting.

'No one's perfect, Paula,' he said quietly.

He took her hand and pulled it towards him, touching her fingers to a place on the lower side of his upper arm, where she could feel a jagged and lumpy scar. 'I fell on a fence when I was ten and tore myself pretty badly under here. And here…' he moved her hand to his waist '…I have a skin spot, a seborrhoeic keratosis, a good half inch across, that feels very rough and scaly. No one's perfect.'

'That's different…'

'I know. But it's a start, isn't it? How do your fingers react to touching those imperfections on my skin? You didn't recoil. Do you think I'm going to recoil from you?'

Slowly he reached out and touched her right breast, making her gasp. The achingly sensitive flesh there responded instantly, tingling and springing into crazed awareness. Her nipple hardened and unconsciously she lifted her ribcage to thrust her breast forward, eager for more of the primitively erotic sensation.

His teasing, rhythmic caress continued, intensified, until he was holding her fully in his hand in between each brushstroke of exploring touch. He widened the gesture and, shockingly, his touch trespassed to the other side of her chest, first just to the stretched flatness of her skin, which was far more sensitive to stimulation than she would have thought, and then, before she had time to recoil, to her scar.

He didn't say anything, didn't prolong the touch, just slid his hand around her ribcage and pulled her into his arms to bury his face in her hair and pillow her head against the quickened beat of his heart.

Paula was dizzy with the newness of it. Parachuting would have been a *breeze,* compared to this! She felt like she *was* parachuting—as if she'd just jumped out of the plane and was free-falling, not yet having pulled the vital ripcord.

It was a sensation, in other words, that could be wonderful if only she could get beyond the panic.

Desperately, she fought to make herself stay in the moment. Max was here, holding her. She could feel her one breast pressed against him, like a small, tender cushion, and could feel the absence of pressure on the other side, which must mean that he could feel it too, yet she could detect no shrinking away, no stiffness in his body at all.

Well, actually, one small amendment there. He was aroused.

The realisation had her pulses beating madly. Holding her like this, feeling her against him, was arousing him! She could even detect a nuance of trembling and the faint, dewy dampness of sweat in the small of his sleekly muscled back, as if he was actually fighting to hold himself back.

A sudden shudder rippled through her and she was close to tears. They burned behind the lids she'd instinctively closed, and if she hadn't held her breath she'd have sobbed aloud. She hadn't expected to know this hectic, sizzling awareness of belonging ever again. She doubted, in this moment, that she'd ever known it so strongly before.

He felt the passion within her and tightened his grip, then groaned and ran his hands down her back, to let them linger lazily on the creamy smoothness of her behind and the tender creases at the top of each thigh.

'I remember these legs, so silky and slender and strong. They seem to go on for ever, and they're so gracefully connected to the rest of you. That evening in Catalina Canyon when I caressed these hollows at the backs of your knees... And how about your arms? The skin there, too... Yes...' He was touching and exploring as he spoke. 'So soft and delicious.'

She shuddered and moaned. She had never realised that her body had so many sensitive, responsive places. Chris had always concentrated on the obvious, zeroing straight in to ravish her breasts until sometimes she had to ask him to stop. Max, though, seemed to have far more eclectic tastes, and she was astonished and set on fire by how *whole* she felt at his touch, and at how complete was his desire for her.

He pulled her to the bed and after this neither of them spoke again. She could scarcely think, either, it seemed, could only feel—a dark, fluid tumult of feeling as everything he had been doing to her gradually coalesced into a building crescendo of ecstasy that spent itself at last, to leave both of them replete and happy and just a little shy.

'So…' he said slowly after a minute, his voice still creaky, a gorgeous sound. 'This is the point at which…'

'At which, what?' she prompted, after he had trailed off into silence again.

'You tell me. Fill in the blank. At which I go home?'

'D-do you, um, need to?'

'*Want* to, you mean?' Cutting through to the truth as usual. 'No! I want to stay!'

'Then stay because that would be…' Lovely. Safe.

'At which we have something to eat, then?'

She laughed. 'Are you hungry?'

'There's a certain craving for ice cream, I admit.'

'I don't have ice cream.' She was absurdly disappointed at having to tell him this.

'Or, on the other hand,' he said immediately, 'crackers and cheese.'

'Those I have.'

'Except that getting out of bed…'

'Yes. It dampens the appetite, doesn't it?' she agreed, feeling decidedly lazy.

'Next time, then, we'll eat before. Or during… Or

we'll have emergency rations already laid out on the bedside table.'

'Next time...' she echoed, testing the idea.

She definitely wanted a next time. If she hadn't expected to want a 'next time' she wouldn't have gone as far as a 'first time'. And yet the idea frightened her somehow, more than she had thought it would. She had expected *this* to be the big hurdle. Telling him. Having him touch her. So shouldn't she be feeling fabulous now, instead of scared?

Max drifted off to sleep a few minutes later, but Paula lay in his arms for a long time, her mind still churning, before she could do the same.

CHAPTER SEVEN

THE alarm. Music blared from the clock radio precisely at six-thirty, and Paula jerked into wakefulness and froze at once. The room was so light already! Surely it wasn't usually this light!

It looked like a classical painting—her pale sheets etched with light and shade where their folds draped and highlighted Max's long body. The yellow glow of morning contoured his hair and his face, gave a sheen to the tanned knobs of his shoulders and showed golden glints at the ends of his dark eyelashes.

As she watched he stirred, and at the exact moment when he opened his eyes she realised that she had missed her one crucial opportunity for escape. Now she was trapped. Naked beneath the sheets, which she'd pulled protectively almost to her chin, she would have to expose herself to him in the moment when she emerged from the bed and crossed the floor to the master bathroom.

No. She couldn't do it.

The 'morning after' was tailor-made for regrets, and if he was having any now, without the blessed concealment of darkness, then the sight of her scarred, incomplete body would have to confront him with the issue in the starkest possible way.

He grunted huskily, rolled his athletic body over, smiled a rumpled, gorgeous smile and squinted at the clock. 'Six-thirty? I think I'll swear...' He did, comprehensively, though mildly, and he grinned at the end of it and was already, in only a few seconds, fully awake. 'I have to go, Paula.'

'Uh-huh...' was all she could manage, still wrapped in the sheets like a mummy, biding her time, loving him like crazy, hating the brightness of day.

'There are some case notes I took home last night that I need today, and I've got hospital patients to see,' he explained.

'You don't have to apologise, Max,' she told him. 'I know how it is, remember?'

She had two or three problem patients scheduled this morning, as well as a visit from the decorator who had been hired to put the finishing touches to the new suite, which would mean her having to sound articulate about colours and finishes. Did she want stencilling? Marbling? Wallpaper borders?

'Breakfast would have been nice, though,' he suggested caressingly. 'In bed, maybe, with neither of us in any hurry.'

He reached out a finger and softly stroked it along her jaw, her neck, her collar-bone...

'It's all right,' she replied quickly, tense. She definitely didn't want him to go any lower. 'We'll...we'll manage that another time.'

'Hope so.' He hesitated for a moment, and she knew he'd noticed that she wasn't exactly responding. One red number on the clock radio silently changed from two to three. Three minutes, already, since the music had started. She could see the wheels turning in his mind, and knew the exact moment when he'd reached a decision—to let her mood go unchallenged. Well, there wasn't time to do anything else, was there?

He slid easily from the bed to sit on its edge and said, more casually than he meant, 'Mind if I grab a shower?'

'Go ahead,' she offered, just as casually. 'There are clean towels in the bathroom.'

'Not going to join me?'

Join him? Oh, God...

'No, I'm going to grab five minutes more snoozing.'

He nodded in an apparently easy acceptance.

An escape! A reprieve. She felt so relieved that she stretched and smiled at him, and felt a wave of heat at the sight of his rippling male body as he loped across the floor.

She waited, almost breathlessly, for the sound of the shower running, and as soon as she heard it she threw back the concealing sheet and hurried to dress, hating the process of inserting her prosthesis into a clean bra, resolutely thinking of other things as she put on underwear and Wedgwood-blue linen pants, carefully avoiding the mirror until she was completely clothed and then making her usual automatic assessment.

Her blouse was sitting right. She looked good. Professional, pretty, and no one would ever guess.

Except that Max didn't have to guess any more. He knew.

There was a difference, though, as the morning light had told her, between *knowing* and actually *seeing*.

A sexual relationship meant more than just one night together, and an emotional relationship meant more than just sex. It meant being comfortable with each other in everything.

Letting him into the bathroom to clean his teeth while I'm having a shower. Bumping into each other in the walk-in closet while we're looking for our underclothes in the basket of clean laundry. Can I do it? Can *he?*

'Trust him!' said her heart.

And then, blessedly, they had a delicious day at work to underpin this inner urging, full of private, shared smiles and silly exchanges of innuendo. She felt as happy as a teenager after her first kiss from a dream date, and wanted to embrace the whole world.

The surly fifteen-year-old with three warts to cauterise couldn't bring her down, nor could the rather supercilious decorator, nor could the over-solicitous new parents who created a scene in the waiting room, and again in her office, over the fact that a four-year-old with a bad cold had come near enough to their precious little Zenith, aged six months, to almost certainly *breathe* on her.

And Max was feeling the same. No prizes for perception there.

His laughter came more readily with Brian and Deborah, and the way he used his body seemed even more athletic and easy than usual. His smile was so dazzling that even in his silver-lensed sunglasses, slipped on as he left the office for lunch, he didn't look distant.

When the mood between them continued into the afternoon Deborah finally commented slyly, 'Can't you spare some of it for the rest of us, you two?'

'Spare what, Deb?' Max returned mildly, while Paula was fully occupied in willing the blush out of her face.

'Whatever health tonic you've both obviously discovered since yesterday. Or tell me the name of it and I'll go out and buy some for myself!'

'You don't really believe happiness comes in a bottle, do you, Deborah?' Max countered reproachfully.

'Aha! So you admit—?'

'We admit nothing.'

His use of 'we' was an admission in itself, of course, and Deborah announced triumphantly, 'OK, guys! That's all I need to know. This may be premature, but I'd better warn you I'm noted for my refusal to attend weddings.'

Unfortunately, she disappeared in to her next patient before either Paula or Max could deny everything in the strongest possible terms. When the door had shut behind her, their gazes locked in shared alarm.

Max made a wry face. 'Should we just go ahead and hire a publicist right now?'

'Sounds as if Deborah's going to do it all for us,' Paula murmured.

'I'm sorry…'

'It's not your fault.'

'I know, but—'

'And I like Deborah. It's just that—'

'Pressure.' He nodded. 'Not what you need, is it?'

'No...'

Thinking back on the conversation as she sat rather tiredly in her new office along the corridor at the end of the day, she decided that the whole exchange might have been fine if it hadn't been for that single final pronoun out of place—'*you* need' instead of '*we* need'—reminding her at just the wrong moment that all this was her problem, not his.

She was the one who had had cancer and lost a breast. He was the one, ultimately, who had to decide what that meant, and whether it made a difference.

The happiness she had felt earlier thinned and evaporated as quickly and easily as spilled water, evaporating from an Arizona sidewalk in the noonday summer sun, but, then again, something inside her urged her to trust him—and she found that she did.

Paula had always liked swimming and swam quite a lot, at beaches or in pools. Here in Zuma she was thinking of joining an athletic club with a pool, and was currently looking at the options. Visiting her newly retired parents in Florida last October, she had lounged around the pool in their retirement complex for hours in her pretty, specially constructed suit that managed to be both fashionably cut and comfortably supportive of her breast prosthesis.

In other words, she had never let the dangers of swimming daunt her and she wasn't going to start now with her swim at Max's, just two days after their poignant and explosive first night together. All the same, beneath her new decisiveness and optimism on the issue, she was still—yes, she had to acknowledge the fact—more than a little self-conscious, more than a little afraid.

The first private time with a man since your first night with him had to be a confronting event in any new relationship. In Paula's situation, there was icing on the cake.

This tremulous self-consciousness hadn't disappeared at six that evening as she arrived at his long, low desert house in the San Ysidro foothills, wearing her swimsuit beneath a slip of a floral sundress and carrying a bag containing something a little dressier to change into later on.

He greeted her at the door in navy swimming trunks, bare feet and an open-necked white sports shirt, and ushered her straight out the back to where his geometric-shaped pool was enclosed on three sides by the cool, elegant sprawl of his house.

'So…' he said, pulling her against him with a capable arm and painting a brief, delicious kiss on her mouth. 'Swim first? Or drink? Or both together?'

'Together?'

'I do have one of those decadent little floating pool chairs with a drink-holder built in to the armrest…'

'Perhaps I can *build* to that,' she suggested, and wasn't entirely joking. 'I'll start with a drink safely on dry land. A gin and tonic, if you've got it.'

It was Dutch courage, and she wasn't even going to pretend to herself that it wasn't. Although could anything have been more reassuring than the way he had greeted her?

'Coming right up,' he said.

He returned with two drinks a few minutes later and scraped a wooden patio chair a little closer to where she was sitting, leaned across to clink their glasses together and proposed a toast. 'To a long, hot summer?'

They both smiled, drank and then lapsed into a silence in which she could actually hear her own heartbeat pulsing against her eardrums. It was her fault. She was in no doubt about that. She was seated in this low, comfortable chair as stiffly as a doll, not even daring to crack a smile because she knew it would be false and if he teased her about it as he'd done before…

I'm not going to be able to do it, she was thinking. I'm just not going to be able to calmly peel off my dress and get into that pool with him watching me, then touching me, because if there's the slightest nuance of regret in his eyes or, worse, if I can see him trying not to look…

He was watching her now, his face half-concealed as he took refuge in his drink, and she knew he must be thinking about their night together, her revelation and the fact that he had touched her in the darkness but had not yet *seen*…

So when hurried feet clicked in percussive heels on the paving stones that led around the house to his side entrance a few minutes later they both turned towards the sound with relief.

'You've invited other people?' she said, not troubling to disguise her thankfulness.

He had got to his feet and was calling on a questioning note, 'Suzanne?'

'Oh, thank goodness you're here, Max!' said a small, dark and very curvaceous woman of about thirty as she emerged from a tangle of bamboo. 'I heard voices out by the pool so I came straight round.'

Voices? Paula wondered. We hadn't spoken for about eight minutes!

'Come through, then,' Max was saying. 'Meet Paula.'

'Paula?' Suzanne frowned.

'Dr Nichols, our new practice partner,' he clarified, and the other woman's brow cleared.

'How great to *meet* you!' she gushed. 'Max mentioned there was a new partner. But, listen, Max.' She bit her lip. 'I'm wondering…'

'Is it Megan?' he seemed unsurprised.

'Yes. Sorry to interrupt. Could you possibly come?' She clasped her hands together beseechingly.

'Of course.'

He was already moving towards her so that the height disparity between them was very apparent. Suzanne was petite and doll-like, and made these attributes into an advantage with her perky white sandals, brief denim shorts and matching halter top. Her upward gaze was long-lashed and just a little too dewy with feminine gratitude for Paula's taste.

Suzanne looked like Barbie in a dark wig...or was that just too bitchy for words? Paula wasn't normally bitchy. Tonight it was purely nerves.

She remained seated and took another reflex sip of her drink, not certain of her role in the little scene until Max turned back to her and said, 'Suzanne's daughter, Megan, has asthma. Suzanne manages it very well, but there are times when she needs a second opinion. Do you mind?'

'Not at all.'

'In fact, if you *really* don't mind, why don't you come too?'

Suzanne didn't look too pleased at this, although she murmured dutifully, '*Two* doctors! I couldn't ask for Megan to be in better hands.'

Max ducked briefly inside to get his stethoscope, then Suzanne led the way back past the bamboo and between some prickly desert plants. It was a path that had been used many times before, and it wasn't quite possible to tell where Max's garden ended and Suzanne's began so that Paula found herself at the side door of the other house with the distinct impression that they could almost be two wings of the same dwelling.

That was very handy for neighbours who got on well.

Inside, eight-year-old Megan was sitting on the couch, leaning forward as many asthmatics did during an attack in order to ease their struggle for breath. She had her nebuliser on the coffee-table beside her and Suzanne said immediately, 'I've had her inhaling like crazy, but it's still pretty bad. She was playing with the cat...'

'Not playing,' Megan wheezed. 'I just said hi... Didn't even...touch him.'

'Now, honey, are you sure?' Suzanne put a hand on her daughter's shoulder. 'You *must* have touched him to be wheezing like this.'

'I didn't!'

'Suzanne,' Max said reproachfully, 'I thought you were going to give the cat away.'

Suzanne made a face. 'Oh, I know, but I just couldn't. Not Misty! He's part of the family. To have him go to strangers... He's an outside cat now, though, Max. He *never* comes inside any more, and Megan knows she's not to touch him.'

'And I didn't!'

'OK, honey...' Suzanne soothed, wringing her hands together nervously. 'Will you have a good look at her Max? Does she need hospital?'

Max bent towards the child, who was a little small for her age, and brought out his stethoscope, but didn't put it to his ears immediately. 'What do you think about giving Misty away?' he asked Megan.

'I'd be sad.'

'I know you would.'

'And cats hate things to be changed.'

'Misty comes over to my place a fair bit. I was thinking it might work if I had him. How about that for an idea?'

'So I could still come and see him?'

'Well, no, because you know that's silly. But he'd have a good home, and he wouldn't have to get upset about moving.'

'Would you really have him, Max?' Suzanne said a little huskily.

'Sure, if you'd like me to.'

'I—I'll have to think about it. It would be an emotional decision.'

'Of course,' Max answered patiently. 'And in the meantime...'

He listened to Megan's chest, talked her through a couple of breathing exercises and asked some questions, but it was clear that the attack was subsiding now. Nothing too dramatic. While understanding a mother's concern, Paula was very privately doubtful that Suzanne would have called a doctor if that had meant doing more than running next door for a free consultation...and from a particularly good-looking single man, at that.

'I don't know why she's getting these attacks still,' Suzanne was complaining. 'She really *doesn't* touch the cat. But we'll just be sitting down, having a snack or something, and boom!'

Paula noticed the cheese-flavoured corn chips on the coffee-table by the nebuliser and asked, 'Were you snacking on these just now?'

'Yes, it's our latest craze, isn't it, Megsie? Two girls alone have to have *some* wicked pleasures!' She gave a frankly saucy look at Max, who smiled back, but Paula wasn't ready to let Suzanne get sidetracked. 'Has she ever been tested for allergy to tartrazine? Suzanne? Max?'

'Tartrazine?' Suzanne echoed blankly.

'Yellow Number Five. It's a very common food dye,' Max explained. 'And it would certainly be in these chips. I'm not actually Megan's doctor so... Has she, do you know, Suzanne?'

Frowning, the other woman shook her head. 'We've been told it was the cat.'

'That doesn't mean something else can't be at work as well,' Max said.

'Oh, no,' Suzanne groaned. 'That would be all I need!'

'It's not too hard to eliminate from your diet, if you're careful,' Paula said. 'And, in fact—'

'Eliminate from *my* diet?' Suzanne tittered. 'Let's get real here!'

'Well, I was going to say, the side-benefit is that it tends to steer you towards foods that are healthier because they're less processed,' Paula continued politely. 'There's no Yellow Number Five in salad or fruit or good-quality wholegrain breads and dairy products.'

'Well, that sounds great, but you won't mind if Mommy cheats a bit, will you, honey?' Suzanne laughed again, turning to her daughter.

'No, Mommy,' Megan said kindly.

'And, of course,' Max said, 'we don't yet know that tartrazine is definitely a problem. Do discuss it properly with Megan's doctor, Suzanne.'

'Oh, I will.' She came up to him and laid a creamy hand on his arm. 'Thanks so much, Max. I don't know what I'll do without you if we move. And if we *don't* move I really think I'll start coming to your practice.'

'Well, my load is very heavy and I'm not taking new patients at the moment myself…'

'Oh, Max…' She pouted prettily.

'But I guess in your case I'd make an exception.'

Suzanne offered them both a drink, her body language conveying the definite impression that she'd wave Paula away with a magic wand if she could, but Max declined smoothly. Suzanne added quickly, 'I'll give you a rain-check, then, since you've got company. Make it tomorrow night?'

'Sure.'

'To thank you, of course, for all the help you give me with Megan. This tartrazine thing, I'm bound to have a hard time over that.'

'Of course I'll help.'

Back by the pool a few minutes later, Max asked in a professional tone, 'So, what did you think?'

Professional tone or not, Paula couldn't help answering rather bluntly, 'I think you're being taken advantage of.'

Only when she'd spoken did she realise how bad it had sounded, and added contritely, 'I'm sorry, that was completely uncalled for. Forgive me, Max. You meant the child's asthma...'

He was grinning. 'I did, but don't apologise. You're right, of course. I'm being very prettily used.'

'You don't mind, I take it?'

'I've given some consideration to minding,' he conceded. 'At first I was given pots of preserves or plates of cookies in return, but that seems to have petered out now. On the other hand, Suzanne is going through a divorce so I'm cutting her some slack. There's talk of a move back to California. She had a realtor in the other day to give her an estimate on the house.

'If the moving idea doesn't go anywhere then, yes, I may retreat to the fortress of my professional position and point out that Megan's own doctor may not appreciate my interference in her case. But,' he pleaded suddenly, on a drawl, 'let's forget about Suzanne, shall we? She's not important.'

Paula didn't realise until the words came that it was just what she'd been waiting to hear. 'Isn't she?'

'Not remotely.' His lips made the words into the promise of a kiss. 'Now, can we take that swim?'

'I'd love to!' she told him, meaning it now.

She meant it, but she'd been nervous before, Max realised. He didn't blame her, he felt something of the same condition himself—a very physical awareness, butterflies in the stomach, no less, that this new state of affairs between them was a long way from being solid. Any relationship had an escape clause built in after the first night. Sometimes people didn't acknowledge that fact. They went on going through the motions for days, weeks...or even the rest of their lives.

But the first night counted. The first night set up patterns and perceptions, expectations and understandings. If the first night was bad then very often the second night never happened. If the first night was good then things shifted gear and got deeper.

And his first night with Paula had been much better than good, except for the huge shock of her revelation. He had really thought, at first, that she was telling him she had cancer—not just had had it once in the past but had it *now,* and his relief when she'd clarified the issue had been immense. But to discover that she'd lost a breast…

He hadn't lied to her. It really hadn't made a difference to what he felt and what he wanted, but if she thought she was the only one who'd been trembling that night she was wrong.

I've got to do this right, he realised, thinking of the minefields that lay ahead in any new relationship, because if I blow it somehow, with the way things are, we just might not get a second chance.

Deliberately casual, he peeled off his shirt…

Paula watched Max dive with smooth seal-like grace into the pool and swim the length of it under water, the sun striking his body through the translucent blue water to show the contrast between the light golden tan on his arms, legs and back and the darkness of his swimsuit.

She took off her dress, thankful that he wasn't watching the action. Had he understood that her confidence was very fragile and new? She entered the water slowly, using the steps, instinctively noting with her peripheral vision that her suit was sitting right and then looking up to find that Max *was* watching her now, stretching his arms along the pool's rim at the far end and lazily kicking.

She moved in the water, which was salt-chlorinated and as smooth as milk, and smiled at him.

Thank goodness she had always had moderate breasts,

which meant that her prosthesis was moderate, too, and didn't tip forward and away from her body, as some women found theirs did in the water. Thank goodness she could afford to invest in special swimwear like this, which was strengthened in the right areas and designed with real care.

All the same, though, she swam a little awkwardly today…

Until Max came up to her a few minutes later, wound cool, wet arms around her and bent his head to seek her lips. 'Gorgeous,' he murmured, the word caressing her mouth.

'Yes, it is, isn't it?' she answered.

'I meant you…'

'Oh, Max…'

'Darling, whatever it is that you're thinking and feeling, *don't!* Feel this, instead…'

And he kissed her until she was breathless and laughing and achingly aroused, then backed off with a teasing grin. 'Um, did I mention I was hoping you'd stay tonight?'

'Well, you didn't, but—'

'You brought your toothbrush anyway?' He grazed her mouth again.

'Actually, I did.'

'Good, then this…' his tongue lapped beneath her earlobe '…is just our preview of coming attractions.'

'I…I think it's going to be a movie I'll enjoy…' But she gave a little shiver.

'Cold?' he asked at once.

'Yes! You're not letting me get any exercise.'

'Sorry,' he grinned, unrepentant.

Paula left the pool, when finally he permitted it, and moved the patio chair to sit in a patch of late sun, finishing off the gin and tonic, until her suit had nearly dried. Max continued to swim back and forth, chewing up the laps with a fluid, powerful crawl that had the pale blue water churning with bubbles, and she gave in to her hungry craving for the sight of his body.

Emerging after fifteen minutes, he glistened with wetness all over until he pressed a thick, boldly coloured towel to his face and rumpled his water-darkened hair into a damp, wayward thicket. Leaving the rest of his body dripping, he reached for his drink and took a long pull, only very slightly out of breath.

'Sorry,' he said. 'I've just left you sitting there.'

'I couldn't take my eyes off you,' she admitted. 'You're so at home in the water.'

'I need it,' he confessed. 'There's rarely a day when I don't swim. Need to work off the job a bit, generally.'

'And since you hate jogging...'

'Yes, we've established that, haven't we?'

Only now did he towel himself all over, and she was mesmerised by the rhythmic action on his supple muscles. 'Getting hungry?' he said.

'Mmm.'

'I thought we'd just get something delivered.'

'That sounds great.'

'Good, because I really didn't feel like sharing you...even with a waiter.'

His touch again, light, caressing, magically banished any of the second-night feelings that threatened to trespass.

Just when did I get this lucky? she wondered, following him into the house. The television was on. He must have had it burbling away in the background before she arrived, using it for company as she sometimes did herself.

'Want to change while I call the restaurant? Chinese?'

'Sounds good.'

'You don't sound as if you care much one way or the other.'

'I don't,' she confessed. 'I'm thinking more about—'

'So am I,' he cut in on a growl.

'Max...' She closed her eyes. They were achingly close to each other.

He lifted his right hand and brought it to her face, then began to trace the tiny lines there with the tip of his forefinger—the faint beginnings of crow's-feet around her eyes, the little tucks near the corner of her lips. Her forehead, too, wasn't free of lines, and he found those as well and caressed them.

'I like a face with just a little history in it,' he whispered at last, and he kissed her, possessing her mouth with the full knowledge of just how much she wanted to respond. 'You're so ripe and real, Paula,' he said against her lips, so that she could feel the caressing heat of his breath. 'The depth in your eyes, the way your mouth just *shows* in its gorgeous shape that it's kissed *and* it's cried...'

She gasped. His hunger for her was throbbingly apparent, and equally apparent was her own reaction to him. There was a pulsing ache all across her lower belly and a shallow rhythm to her breathing. Like the other night, too, her right nipple had tightened into a hot little bud, making her so aware of what was missing, and she knew that it would simply take time before she got so used to this that she forgot about it.

'Paula, can the Chinese wait?' he growled roughly, and she trembled with the strength of their shared response to each other. 'Because I can't...'

But Kelly Rainer's voice cut across his, intrusive after the music of a commercial. Max pulled himself away with a muttered oath and lunged for the coffee-table by the couch.

'Now, to recap tonight's main stories...' the Channel Six news anchor began, and was suddenly blasted out of existence by Max's finger on the remote control.

'Gee, you really don't like that woman, do you?' Paula teased lightly, thinking of his tense exchange with the gorgeously groomed Kelly last Friday night at the hospital.

There was a beat of significant silence. Max's eyes remained fixed on the blank grey screen of the television, then he said slowly, 'I wouldn't say I didn't like her… You know I'm divorced… Kelly is my ex-wife.'

There was no real reason for it to be a shock, but somehow it was. Perhaps it was part of the phenomenon of the modern celebrity. Paula had Kelly Rainer in her living-room most nights of the week, telling her the news.

It created an intimacy, a sense that she knew the glamorous personality, and to find that she'd once been such an intimate part of Max's life was jarring—much more difficult than some anonymous creature safely removed to another city or another social orbit with no connection to Paula's own. Not to mention, of course, the fact that, physically, Kelly was so very, very perfect…

'Should I have told you before?' Max was asking quietly.

'No… No, not at all,' she managed, meaning it.

'But it's a problem…'

'*No!* But I do need to…get my head around it.'

'Channel Ten has a very good news team, too,' he drawled.

She laughed. 'Oh, Max…'

'Wasn't that what you were thinking?' he pressed, wearing a crooked smile. 'That you'd been entertaining her unawares in your own home?'

'Can you teach me how you do that, please?'

'Do what?'

'Read my mind.'

'Oh, that? It's not difficult. You have an autocue scrolling across your forehead.' He came up and kissed her there. 'Seriously, shall we talk about Kelly?'

'Seriously? I—' But before she could answer him his pager, lying forgotten on the small wooden table that held her drink, began to pipe, and she turned to it with a sound of frustration. 'You're on call?'

'Yes,' he muttered. 'Let's hope it's something extremely non-urgent. I'll deal with it at once, get it out of the way.'

'Yes, do.'

He strode across to the phone to call his answer service, turning away from the instrument a couple of minutes later with the news that Lisa Carey had called in, sounding distraught.

'Call her,' Paula said.

He was already keying in the number, only as his silent wait lengthened it was clear he wasn't getting an answer.

With Lisa's health insurance company placing strict limits on the length of hospital stay it would cover, the new mother of quads had been discharged from the maternity ward yesterday. Georgia, the biggest and healthiest of her babies, had joined her at home today now that she had begun to record a good weight gain, following the initial drop after birth.

Max and Paula had both seen the Carey quads in hospital in the five days since their birth, taking it in turns to make the daily visit and liaising closely with the hospital special care nursery and N.I.C.U., which were responsible for the babies until their discharge. Tiny Alex's condition was still touch-and-go, although there had been no serious setbacks, and Hayley and Audrey were doing well but would remain in hospital until each weighed over four pounds and showed no other cause for concern.

Georgia, then, was the only baby that Lisa would have at home with her for several more weeks, and she had been on tenterhooks lest something should prevent the little girl's discharge this morning. Nothing had, but now…

'I hope to hell it's not something serious,' Max muttered, 'but I'm not taking any chances. I'll go round there, I think. Why isn't she picking up the phone?'

'Gone to the hospital?'

'Yes, perhaps. I'll ring them from the car phone and find out. Are you coming?'

'Of course!'

'Thought so...' The understated drawl contained a confidence in their connection which filled her with heat and gave her a refreshed certainty that she wasn't a fool to hold hope for their future.

They were in his car a minute later, and Paula made the call to the hospital as Max pulled out of the driveway.

'No, no Mrs Carey or baby Carey has come in, Dr Nichols,' said a weary, uninterested voice on the other end of the line, half-swamped with background noise from the busy emergency department.

'Thank you,' Paula responded, then relayed the news to Max.

'Don't know if that's good news or bad news,' was his drawled comment.

He had looked up the Careys' address in the telephone directory before setting out, and now tossed his Zuma street map across to Paula and asked her to verify his route. It wasn't far, another five minutes.

Curtis Carey answered their knock with a strained expression. 'I've just been calling your service. You never called back.'

'I did, straight away. There was no answer.'

'God, it must have been when we were in the bathroom. Had the faucets running and didn't hear. It never occurred to me. Because I wasn't expecting you to call back that soon.'

'But what's wrong, Curtis?' Max didn't wait for an invitation into the house, and Paula followed closely in his wake.

'She vomited blood, and her diaper was full of black

stuff. I wanted to take her straight to the hospital but Lisa doesn't want to panic. The baby seems fine… I mean, she's not crying or hot or anything. Lisa thinks they'll put Georgia back in hospital if they think we can't manage…'

'OK, let's take it slowly,' Max soothed. 'Lisa's upstairs with Georgia?'

'Yes, she's trying not to come up and down until she's less sore.' He was leading the way to the stairs as he spoke. 'They're here, Lisa,' he called. 'Dr Costain and Dr Nichols. They're coming up.'

'Oh, thank God!' That comment told them her effort not to panic hadn't quite succeeded.

'Now, firstly…' Max began. They had reached the bedroom, where Lisa was sitting up in bed with tear-stained cheeks as she held the tiny baby who was asleep, apparently without a care in the world. Paula took her very gently and noted her breathing, pulse and colour. The first two were fine, but the last was not quite right. Georgia stirred and snuffled a little, but didn't wake.

'Lisa, you've been breast-feeding, right?' Max said in the meantime.

'Yes, my milk took a while to come in, but today I started expressing some to supplement the girls in hospital. Alex isn't ready for it yet.'

'And are you sore?'

'Very!'

'Actually cracked?'

'Yes. It's so painful!'

'Then Georgia vomiting blood is nothing to worry about, although I know it must have scared you. That's your blood, and she can't digest it so she brings it back up. You weren't shown a nipple-care routine in hospital?'

'There wasn't time! A nurse mentioned something… I was exhausted, I didn't take it in…'

'You'll just have to ride the soreness out, then, I'm

afraid. Perhaps hold off on expressing for a few days, if that seems to be making it worse.'

'And it helps to rub your nipples with colostrum and milk after each feed, Lisa,' Paula came in.

'Now, the black stool in her diaper, too, is just the last of the bowel contents that were there before birth. Now that your milk is fully in and has had time to work through her system, her next movement should be like yellow curds, with no unpleasant odour.'

'So we were panicking for no reason, and we got you here for nothing...'

'That was my decision,' Max said firmly, 'and I'm quite happy about it.'

Paula took advantage of the small pause that followed to swing gently towards him, the baby still cradled carefully in her arms. Georgia was so tiny! Just four pounds three ounces on discharge this morning. Frighteningly small to have at home! 'Have a look,' she said neutrally to Max, and he saw at once what bothered her about the baby.

'She's looking a cute shade of yellow, isn't she?' he said with deceptive good cheer to the Careys, and they both nodded.

'That's normal, isn't it?' Lisa said. 'We were told so. Apparently they don't worry so much about jaundice these days.'

'Not as much as they should sometimes,' he answered. 'I'd like you to bring her in tomorrow and we'll do a simple test.'

'You mean...?' The alarm was suddenly back in their faces. They'd been through a lot, these two, over the past months, and it wasn't over yet.

'Don't worry,' Max soothed. 'There's something building in her blood called bilirubin, and if it gets too high and stays too high it can have serious consequences. A tiny baby like this can't get rid of the bilirubin as quickly as she should so I would like to test its levels. If they are too high there are simple things we can do, such as giving treatment under lights, that should bring it within safe limits. I'm sure you understand when I say I'd like to err on the side of caution.'

'Oh, absolutely,' Lisa answered. 'If anything goes wrong with any of them...' Her voice faltered and she began to cry. 'I'm sorry.'

'It's tough,' Max murmured.

'Her mom arrives from California tomorrow, and she'll stay as long as we need her,' Curtis said. 'Even if that's a year! My mom and dad are here in Zuma...'

'And my sister is at home, just a few streets away, with a two-year-old,' Lisa added. 'We'll have plenty of help. I just want them all healthy and home from the hospital!'

'Of course you do, and we're all working towards that. Curtis, why don't you call our office first thing in the morning and make an appointment for that test? Are you going in to the N.I.C.U. tonight to see the bubs?'

'Definitely!' Curtis answered, 'And Lisa will spend as much time as she can there tomorrow.'

A few minutes later Max and Paula had left the Careys' spacious split-level house and were on their way down the brick driveway. With a large, landscaped and well-fenced rear yard, it would be a delightful home for four children once these difficult early months were past.

'I'm glad we went,' Max said, 'because I strongly suspect that jaundice will need treatment.'

'And in their position they didn't need a trek down to the emergency room over a false alarm. I quite understand why they panicked at the sight of vomited blood!'

'Now, are you as hungry as I am?' he said lightly as they regained his car.

'Probably hungrier.'

Good food, a little wine, some music... Just one phone call from a worried parent at nine p.m., which was quickly dealt with. Some long, delectable kisses on the couch, and then bed, and a long, delectable night of love-making and curled-up-together sleep… The subject of Kelly Rainer didn't come up again, and things were so good, so very, very good that, for now anyway, Max's ex-wife really didn't matter.

CHAPTER EIGHT

'MAX...'

'Yes, sweetheart?'

'I think...we know each other well enough by now that I can tell you this,' Paula began slowly. She felt him stiffen.

'Tell me what?' he queried warily.

They were seated together on her peach leather couch after a casual meal at home, watching television. Or, at least, Max would have considered that they were watching television. Paula had a different opinion.

'I mean,' she hedged carefully. 'It's often the *little* things that—'

'Paula!' Now it was an ominous growl.

'You want me to cut to the chase?'

'Please!'

'OK, then.' Without warning, she lunged across his body and snatched the remote control from his grasp, before saying in a satisfied voice, 'There!'

'Wh—?'

'The channel-surfing, Max, the channel-surfing,' she intoned. 'From now on, whether we're here or at your place, *I* am in charge of the remote and that's a non-negotiable position!'

He had the grace to look shame-faced, having spent the past five minutes switching back and forth between the movie they'd started to watch, the basketball match that was approaching an exciting finish and the prime-time offerings of several other channels. 'I know it's a horrible habit,' he admitted.

'Habit?' Paula echoed indignantly. 'It's right up there

with ‘‘Thou shalt not covet thy neighbour’s ox’’, as far as I’m concerned.’

‘You never said…’

‘No, but haven’t you wondered why you always find it carefully hidden beneath a magazine at my place?’

‘Nope!’ He grinned. ‘I found that irritating, sure. It was one of the things I was going to mention when I thought we knew each other well enough. ‘‘Paula…’’ Very tactfully, of course. ‘‘Could you please, for my sake, if we mean anything to each other, *not* store your remote under a magazine?’’’

‘Oh, Max…’ She collapsed in a fit of giggles which were so thoroughly drowned by his kiss that she didn’t even notice when he stole the remote control back again and extinguished the television altogether.

It was just over five weeks now since their explosive and emotional first night together. Five weeks of shared, unspoken realisation that each minute they spent together only deepened what they’d already begun to feel so strongly.

Their involvement was an open secret at the practice and, though they made a point of not lunching together more than once a week, they spent several nights a week in each other’s company from the end of one working day until the start of the next.

Max was wonderful to be with. It wasn’t that they did anything particularly inventive or outlandish together, but somehow he seemed to know the quietest and quirkiest restaurants, the coolest, coziest cinemas and the nicest times of day for walking a desert hiking trail or shopping at an offbeat antique mall.

He wasn’t perfect, of course. What man was? Max’s dire failings thus far included liking oysters *au naturel, not* liking opera and then, of course, he had that maddening problem with the remote control. But he was an amazing man and he already belonged in Paula’s life in a way that she’d never expected to find.

Working with him gave a further grounding to what they each felt. Most of their workload, of course, brought little shared contact over patients, but the Carey quads continued to need their joint attention. Georgia remained the healthiest of the four, but Hayley had gone home last Friday, with oxygen equipment in tow, and Audrey would, they hoped, follow her two sisters within the next week.

Lisa was very eager for this, particularly as Alex continued to suffer setbacks which slowed his progress and Curtis needed tactful handling at times as his support for his wife had threatened to become over-aggressive on several occasions. It was a long, slow, anxious time for the Careys, and Max and Paula shared the job of staying in close and regular contact with the couple and their babies.

If there was one thing that troubled Paula about their deepening relationship, it was that Max was being almost too careful with her. She'd almost said to him a few days ago, 'You don't need to treat me like you treat Curtis Carey. I'm a grown-up, and I'm reasonably secure. I can handle an impatient word or a confronting talk.' But she'd held the words back, realising in time how grateful she was to have a man who was capable of this sensitivity, even when she felt she didn't need it.

And, if she was honest, there were times when she *did* need it. They still, for example, made love only in the dark. The sense of vulnerability in her had lessened markedly, and when they dressed in the mornings she was far more relaxed than she had been at first, but he still hadn't seen her completely naked in full light and she knew it was something she'd have to get to gradually.

Nor had they talked about Kelly Rainer. Perhaps, from his perspective, there simply wasn't a lot to say. It had been a short and not very successful marriage, and it was over. There were no children, and as both had careers of comparable success in their different fields there had been no acrimonious division of assets and property.

So why do I have this nagging feeling that something about Kelly is important? Paula wondered inwardly as she nestled against Max's side on the couch.

His lips trailed down from her earlobe to her collarbone but she was distracted now, no longer lost in his touch as she groped for an answer. A sense that...that she isn't finished with me. That she's going to shadow my life somehow. But, no! That's ridiculous!

'You're not thinking about the irresistible onslaught of my manliness on your senses any more, are you, Paula?' came a low, masculine growl.

'Hmm?'

'I *said*...' Max repeated the question with an even more ironic twist to his tone, and Paula bit her lip. He was right, of course.

'Sorry...'

'I guess you're wondering about the final score of the Bulls versus Lakers game, huh?'

'That, and the endings of *Pretty Woman* and *The Rock*, and how to put the roof on the do-it-yourself garden gazebo, and—'

'OK, OK,' he laughed. 'I hereby swear never to channel-surf in your presence again, provided we resume this activity...' he brushed his mouth against hers '...at some later point in the evening.'

'Not *too* much later,' she murmured, looking at him languorously through her lashes. 'And, if we're making promises, I'll meet you halfway. I hereby promise to try oysters *au naturel* next time we eat out.'

'Speaking of which...' He clapped a hand to the side of his head.

'Oysters?'

'Eating out. My sister and her husband have invited us to a barbecue at their place on Sunday. Can you make it?'

'Definitely,' Paula answered at once. 'I'd like to meet your sister very much...'

There had been something significant in the way Max had talked about her meeting his sister that told Paula it was important.

That made sense, she supposed. She already knew that Max's family was important to him—that his parents phoned him or came up from Tucson regularly, that he was wild about his nieces and that he was almost chivalrous in his protectiveness towards Janey.

There was the nuance of a suggestion that Janey hadn't had an easy life, but Paula didn't know the details, and in the three days that led up to the planned barbecue at Janey's house on Sunday evening she was too concerned with her own fear about somehow not measuring up—loving sisters could be critical, she understood—that she didn't spend much time wondering about Janey herself.

She was content to know that if Janey was in any way a female version of Max then she would like her. On the other hand, of course, a female version of Max might also possess high standards when judging any woman who presumed to want to be a part of Max's life.

When they pulled up in the driveway of Janey and John Owens' spacious-looking Spanish-style house on the far side of the San Ysidro Mountains, therefore, she found that she was feeling distinctly nervous.

John's and Janey's two teenage daughters, each with a friend, were already splashing and shrieking in the pool and using the slide that fed into the deep end, and the man who had to be John Owens was in a wet bathing suit as well as he prepared the charcoal in a big barbecue grill which stood in the shade of the vine-covered pergola that half surrounded the pool.

'As I told you, informal and family-style,' Max said, climbing out of the car. 'Hope that's OK.'

'Just what I feel like.'

'Janey'll be in the kitchen, making a couple of fabulous salads,' he predicted, 'but I'll introduce you to John on the way up.'

He did so, bringing her up to the barbecue just as John touched a match to the fluid-soaked charcoal. There was a flare of flame and Paula leaned back quickly.

'Whoops! How are those eyebrows?' John said at once. 'Nice and toasted? Sorry!'

'That's all right,' she said with a laugh. 'They were getting a bit bushy anyway.'

'That doesn't seem likely, I have to tell you,' was John's opinion, as he reached out to shake hands, after a quick wipe on his shorts to get off the smear of charcoal dust. Paula liked him at once.

'Janey's inside?' Max said.

'Swearing at her recipe book,' John confirmed.

'Oh, it's misbehaving?'

'She was wanting to know who on earth would have one teaspoon of duck fat just lying around their kitchen.'

'I can see her point,' Paula commented.

'So she decided to use olive oil instead.'

'In that case, maybe the storm has passed and it's safe for us to go up,' Max concluded.

'Storm?' John laughed. 'You know Janey. She rarely gets worse than a sun-shower.'

He went back to his charcoal and Max led Paula up a flight of stone-flagged steps that opened onto a terrace and then an air-conditioned kitchen and family room. A rather small woman in a short-sleeved lemon shirt stood at the counter-top with her back to them, leaning to hold down the top of an electric blender which was churning a salad dressing so noisily that she hadn't heard them enter.

When it stopped Max said, 'Hi, Janey.' She whirled around in shock, but Paula had to mask a shock of her own.

Janey Costain Owens had burn scars on both arms, running from her fingers to her neck and jaw. Not recent ones, by any means. The accident must have happened some years ago, but her skin retained the texture and appearance of melted plastic in many places and would be that way for life.

It took only a moment for the shock to ebb on both sides. 'You scared me,' Janey scolded, then came forward to hug her brother, her mobility unimpeded by the damage to her skin. 'Hi, big guy! And this, of course, must be—'

'Paula,' she supplied, and Janey hugged her as well.

In the brief contact Paula just had time to be aware of the scarred texture of Janey's arms and the unusual tautness of the skin in some places. With burns of this extent, she must have had many weeks of pain in hospital and probably more than one follow-up operation to prevent the scars from contracting and restricting her movement. She'd probably needed cosmetic surgery to her lower face as well.

Clearly, however, the long-ago accident had not been allowed to shadow her life.

'This is a classically dreadful thing to say,' came her bright voice, 'but, heaven help me, I'm going to say it anyway! It's lovely to meet you because Max has told us so much about you! There! And it *was* dreadful, wasn't it? Now you're all embarrassed!'

'I can take it, I think.' Paula smiled.

'Doesn't this happen to you, though?' Janey went on, beguiling in her frankness. 'Don't you find yourself telling other people's children how much they have *grown* since you last saw them? Even though you hated it as a child when people said it to you? Or telling old school friends that they haven't changed a bit, and *believing* it, even though they couldn't possibly have been that wrinkled twenty years ago?'

'That's the trouble with clichés,' Paula agreed. 'They're usually true!'

'And often so much what you're actually thinking that you can't pretend you're not. Children *do* grow incredibly fast, and I *was* dying to meet you because of hearing about you from Max. Now, is it too soon to dress this salad?'

She peered out of the window and down to where John was still orchestrating the layout of his coals. 'Yes,' she decided. 'It'll be an hour before we eat and my lettuce will go translucent. OK, in that case, what will you have to drink? Or will you swim first?'

'I'll swim. And then I'll help.'

'And so will I,' Max said with a lazy smile.

Paula caught his glance and accurately read his contentment. As a mind-reader, she wasn't yet quite in his class but she was starting to know him now.

He approved of her reaction to Janey. And he told her with the heat and depth of his expression that, yes, the fact that Janey was badly scarred had been important in making him who he was—a man who looked beyond physical imperfections to what lay beneath. He might once have been married to the very perfect Kelly Rainer, but perfection wasn't all he knew about.

Her swelling sense of trust in their relationship grew a little more.

'Why didn't you tell me about Janey's accident?' she asked Max after their swim, when they were both lazing on pool-side lounging chairs in the pergola's semi-shade. Chicken and burgers were sizzling on the grill and John had gone inside to help Janey bring out the salads, dishes, silverware and condiments, while the girls, Tara and Connie, were giggling with their friends at the far end of the pool.

'About the fact that she's scarred?' Max said.

'Yes. Like I am.'

'Because I think showing is better than telling,' he

answered. 'It would have sounded crass and superficial, wouldn't it? Like when someone says, ''Some of my best friends are Jewish,'' or whatever it might be to counter an accusation of prejudice.'

'I guess it would,' she conceded.

'And I would have hated to use my sister in that way, as a tribute to my own—what?'

'Open-mindedness? Sensitivity?' Paula suggested.

'I guess,' he agreed. 'Janey is my sister, and we're close, and I wanted you to meet her. I hoped, yes, that you would be encouraged by the meeting, and that it would make you see—'

'It does,' she told him quickly. 'It does, Max.'

They didn't talk about it any more. They didn't need to. Paula went in to dress again in her matching apricot shorts and blouse, and then helped John and Janey to bring out the last of the barbecue things. The meal was delicious, with a tangy bite to the marinated chicken and a crisp freshness to the inventive salads Janey had made.

'Have to say, though,' Max commented mildly, 'I think this one with the mushrooms really would have been better with that teaspoon of duck fat...'

Janey pelted him with a hamburger bun.

'There's cheesecake for dessert,' she said a little later, 'which John made, so he's exempted from cleaning up, and so are the girls as they've got friends here.'

'I'll help,' Paula offered at once, following through on her earlier offer.

And she knew that the trap had been set for her quite deliberately even before Janey said to her inside at the sink, 'Now that I've got you alone, Paula, I'm going to ask you all sorts of terrible questions.'

'Go ahead!'

'Really?'

'Well, you said it as if I didn't have a choice.'

'But you do, of course. That's the thing about being

brazen. It's supposed to signal your willingness to be told to mind your own business.'

'Actually,' Paula said slowly, 'I'd feel very happy if it turns out that it *is* your business.'

Janey gave a little skip of pleasure. 'You mean you're in love with my brother? *Awwright!*' Then she suddenly got serious. 'I was really, really, *really* hoping you'd say that because he needs someone like you.'

'What do you mean, someone like me?' Another pediatrician? Someone without a breast? Impossible that she should mean *that.* For a start, did she even know?

'Well, even though I liked Kelly—you know about Kelly, right?'

'That they were married, but that's about it.'

'They just weren't right for each other, that's all. After the pretty difficult relationship he had with Stephanie—Damn! Do you know about her?'

'He's mentioned her.'

'Good, because I'm not very good at keeping secrets. Anyway, Max and Stephanie split up years ago, of course, but after her he didn't want another doctor. At the time he blamed the fact that he and Stephanie were both doctors for why it didn't work out. It *wasn't* that, of course.'

'No?'

'No! Stephanie was nothing *but* a doctor, that was the trouble. Whereas you—I hear you've taken up pottery.'

Paula groaned. 'He really *has* told you all about me, hasn't he?'

'He has.' Suddenly Janey was serious. 'I—hope that's all right.'

'You mean...?'

'I mean the cancer. And your breast.'

'It's fine,' Paula answered, meaning it.

'He won't have told anyone else, but he and I do have our heart-to-hearts.'

'Kelly, though...' Paula prompted.

'Kelly, yes,' Janey reminded herself. 'They met when she was doing a story on attention deficit disorder.' Paula knew by this time that this was one of Max's professional interests. 'And I think it was a classic case of attraction of opposites, with them being from such different worlds. They married too quickly—which I blame Stephanie for. Max feels guilty, though, that he could have been so mistaken about his feelings for Kelly. That's why he doesn't like to be reminded of his marriage.'

'I see...'

'The thing is, Stephanie had stalled on marriage for so long and then made so many conditions—that Max had to move to Minnesota, that there would be no children. With Kelly, he couldn't believe it was so easy, and he mistook that easiness for love. He isn't the first person to have done it!'

'And yet, easy or not, it didn't last.'

'That's the trouble when opposites attract. The oppositeness—that isn't a word—lasts, but the attraction doesn't. He works early, she works late. She's as glamorous and put-together as they come, he likes women with a natural look. Like you.'

'Oh.'

'Seriously! Kelly drove him nuts, spending an hour and a half getting dressed up to go out.'

'But if underneath...'

'Yes, I agree, things like that can be worked out. But the real crunch was that Kelly didn't want children.'

'Oh.'

'And you can't blame Max for not finding that out *before* the wedding because at that stage she'd told him she did. She would still claim she does, too, only her timeframe for it is so long and extended. She's only twenty-nine now, and Max is eleven years older,' Janey explained brightly, while Paula's ears rang.

'She wanted to wait until her career had really consolidated and peaked. Late thirties, she talked about, which would have made Max nearly fifty, and he just didn't want to wait that long, knowing that fertility declines with age and fearing that some other career goal would come up for her that was too important to miss and she'd put it off even longer.'

'And Max wants kids…that badly?' Paula had to fight to make her voice sound normal.

Children. She had been struggling with so many other issues in their growing relationship that she hadn't even got as far as this biggest issue of all.

'Oh, yes!' Janey said, absorbed in cleaning out her blender, which was a finicky, difficult task. There *was* some stiffness from the scarring on her hands, Paula saw.

Janey hadn't noticed the change in Paula's expression.

Or else I'm keeping it to myself better than I think…

'Max wants kids pretty badly,' Janey continued. 'It'd be odd for a pediatrician *not* to, don't you think?' She looked up for a moment.

'Oh, yes,' Paula agreed. 'It would.'

She wanted children herself. She always had. Only for the past five years she had put that desire very carefully aside and had told herself that it was enough to be able to celebrate her own life after those dreadful days and weeks when she'd faced the realistic fear of death.

And, thanks to modern medicine, death had been staved off, hopefully for another thirty or forty years, but modern medicine had its price.

Chemotherapy could cause sterility.

Her menstrual cycle had resumed some months after the end of the treatment five years ago, but it hadn't gone back to the way it had been before. Her periods were erratic, infrequent and short. She was thirty-six now, and at that age fertility was starting to become an unknown quantity anyway.

'I've already asked Max to accept so much about me, and now I'd be asking for this, too—that he accept the strong possibility that I'd never be able to have his child.'

The knowledge seemed to sit in her stomach like a heavy meal—immovable, uncomfortable, horrible. She was too miserable about it to even face it, let alone decide what action it commanded from her. Also, she was in the midst of people with whom she had to maintain the appearance of enjoying herself.

Not just people, either, but Max's delightful sister, her husband and their happy teenage girls—a family whom, earlier, she'd been testing out in her mind as future relatives.

'Ready for my masterpiece?' John asked, coming in from the terrace.

Paula's mind went blank. *Masterpiece?* All she could think of at the moment was this new issue in her relationship with Max, coming to the fore on a day when she'd felt so good about their future.

'The cheesecake,' he prompted.

'Mmm, yes!' She manufactured what was meant to be a greedily appreciative smile. Thank goodness Max had stayed out by the pool because he would have seen through it before it even reached completion.

On the subject of completion, Janey seemed satisfied with their talk and content for it to end. Paula got the distinct impression, which ought to have been gratifying, that she had successfully passed Janey's stringent yet tactfully conducted test.

In other circumstances she would have been warmed and rather delightfully amused at the notion, knowing that she'd been conducting tests of her own. Now, though...

Max has been let down by two women already—women he cared about enough to form serious relationships with. What would it do to our relationship, years down the track, if I let him down again? All along I've been thinking it was my lost breast that might drive us apart, but I've been wrong. There are more important issues at stake...

The cheesecake was delicious, heaped with fresh fruit, rich, light but not too sweet, and the coffee was just as good. Paula put her inner questioning aside, knowing that this wasn't the place or the time to think about it properly or reach any sort of conclusion.

They left fairly early, at around nine. When Max swung confidently into her driveway he asked lazily, 'Am I coming in?' There was clearly only one answer he wanted.

She gave it, while wondering if it would have been stronger and better to have sent him home.

But she *didn't* want to spend the rest of the evening alone! She wanted him!

And he wanted her too. He made no secret of it, sliding his hand seductively down her back as they entered the house then leaning across to make a hot, teasing trail along her neck with his mouth.

'There's just one problem,' he said. 'I haven't managed to get to the pharmacy department at the supermarket today for a fresh supply of certain protective—'

'It doesn't matter,' she told him distractedly, bitterly aware today of the deeper truth of her words. 'It's a safe time of the month.'

It was all too likely that *any* time was safe...

Over the past few weeks, she had loved the fact that he was so conscientious about contraception, and had told him so, which he'd appreciated. How the best men glowed in just the right, deceptively offhand way after a sincere and well-delivered stroking to the ego! She'd loved that.

Now she started to wonder if she'd given the wrong impression. If, as a result, he thought she had good reason to believe she was fertile...

'Max,' she began desperately, 'there's something we need to talk about.'

'No, there isn't.'

He kissed her into silence, but she fought him off...*tried* to fight him off. He kept turning it into a caress or an excuse to deliciously imprison her arms.

'We *must.*'

'We must make love first.'

'No.' She was trying to stop him, hold him still here in the hall, but somehow that wasn't happening. He was coaxing her inexorably towards the bedroom.

'Do you know how much better it is when we talk *afterwards?*' he demanded, half teasing, half serious. His hands seared her skin. 'Your voice gets all deep and vibrant and syrupy,' he teased seductively, 'and you say things when we're touching naked, beneath the sheets, that you'd never say during a restaurant meal or a quick breakfast before work.'

'But—'

'This is your tight voice, your, "When I tell Max this he's going to immediately forget my telephone number" voice.'

They had reached the bedroom door.

'Janey thought you were great,' he said huskily. '*I* thought you were great, and you looked fabulous in that swimsuit. Can't *tell* you what your delicious rear end does to me at the top of those long, long legs.'

'Please—'

They were inside the bedroom. He was pulling her onto the bed.

'My darling...my darling...'

A hot, urgent kiss punctuated each seductive, caressing phrase.

'Oh, Max...'

He rolled onto her, supporting his torso with his elbows, and swooped down to claim her mouth and ravage it with shameless hunger. Paula's strength failed her completely and she felt tears prick behind her eyes.

Oh, God, I love him! I love him so much! And if

what he shows is what he feels, then maybe... He began to slide her shorts down past her slim hips. Maybe that will be enough.

There was an explosive tenderness in their lovemaking that night that went beyond even the heights they had reached together before. Perhaps there *was* a difference when you didn't use contraception. She felt almost painfully close to him, stirred to her utmost depths by the primal beauty of this strongest of connections, as if they'd reached an even deeper meeting point than before.

When they both stilled at last, after what could have been hours, she knew that silent tears were coursing down her cheeks. He knew it, too. He could taste them.

'Paula...?'

'Happy,' she said, and it was true because, whatever came next, she had at least known *this*.

'Good.'

He burrowed possessively against her until she was cradled in his arms exactly as he wanted, then fell asleep there as if he was comfortable enough to stay for the rest of his life.

I'll talk to him about it tomorrow night, she decided. He has to know that I might be infertile before it becomes just too unfair.

Perhaps it was hardly surprising that Paula was even more aware of Max than usual at work the next day. They met up on the maternity floor at the hospital, in the neonatal intensive care unit, where Paula was seeing a newborn patient, the baby brother of a three-year-old whom she'd seen once for a well check-up and once for an ear infection.

Little Michael's problems weren't serious, although it had taken quite a bit of effort to reach that conclusion, and his parents, Bill and Judy Klinger, were understandably wrung out and anxious by this time.

Like Georgia Carey, Michael had developed unacceptably high bilirubin levels during his first day of life and had been put through a range of tests to exclude the possibility of a serious cause. As Paula would be seeing him from now on for all his routine care, she had had to consult with the hospital neonatologist and other professionals in the hospital team in order to come up with the clearest and most accurate summary of the baby's condition to present to the Klingers.

Now, at seven-thirty in the morning, the Klingers stood beside Michael's transparent plastic isolette, clearly making a conscious effort to ignore the other babies that surrounded him who were, in many cases, much more seriously ill.

With the Careys' experience still so fresh in Paula's mind, although Alex had now graduated from the section of the unit that contained the sickest babies, she was very aware of just how bewildering this place could be.

Ill babies. It was a frightening sight to most people, and as she approached the Klingers Paula saw Max with two more parents several yards away, clearly helping them through a similar ordeal. She glimpsed Lisa Carey, too, on her way in to visit Alex at the far end of the unit.

'The good news,' she told the Klingers at once, 'is that you should have him home with you very soon now.'

Mrs Klinger immediately started to cry, lowering her face so that wings of rather tired blonde hair concealed her reddened eyes. Mr Klinger blinked behind wire-framed glasses and nodded cautiously.

'That means...there's no real problem? Everything's fine?'

'It's going to be,' Paula answered. 'It's been a scary few days for you, hasn't it?'

'Yes, with the toxaemia to start with,' Mrs Klinger said, 'before I even delivered.'

'And then no one *telling* us,' Mr Klinger said indignantly. 'No one would *say* what they suspected. That makes me very angry, actually.'

'And yet to have worried you for nothing...' Paula pointed out. 'There were several quite serious things which could have been going on and which had to be ruled out. Cystic fibrosis, for a start.'

'Oh, no!'

'And it *has* been ruled out,' she hastened to say.

Michael had been found to have a bowel plugged by meconium, the black tar-like stool that was present in the bowel before birth. This could have several different causes, some of which could be fatal, and the meconium plug in turn was probably what had caused his jaundice—which could also lead to a serious brain condition called kernicterus that resulted in profound retardation if left unrecognised and untreated. There was also a rather serious thing called Hirschsprung's disease...

It was a minefield of sequential possibilities, therefore, some of them so rare that you couldn't possibly inflict days of anguish on parents by explaining them all on the slight chance that one of them would be found.

'If I can try to summarise it all for you,' she went on.

'Please do!' Mr Klinger said.

'The drug that you were given, Mrs Klinger, to control your dangerously high blood pressure—'

'The toxaemia?'

'Yes. That is what we are now convinced caused the meconium plug. That in turn prevented your baby's system from dealing with the bilirubin as it should so the level built up until it was unacceptably high. He's been put on phototherapy now, as I think you've been told by the nurses.'

'Well, the special lights...'

'Yes, I guess you can't miss them.' She smiled. 'The light treatment will be continued for a few more days, while Michael is carefully monitored to check its effect, and then he'll be ready to go home.'

'A few more days! That sounds so long...' Mrs Klinger said, getting teary again. 'It was so hard, going home without my baby.'

'I know, and with you yourself feeling tired and sore and finding it difficult to walk. But now you can visit him as much as you like, even stay round the clock if you want to, and you can feed him as you've been doing.'

The Klingers had several more questions, which were easy to answer, then Paula said, 'So I'll see him for his first office visit at the end of next week.'

'I can't wait,' Mrs Klinger said, turning back to her baby.

Max was still totally focused on the parents of the other baby, a tiny premature girl. They seemed quite upset, angry and anxious, and clearly had a lot of questions which weren't nearly as easy to respond to as the Klingers' had been.

Paula went to the nurses' station to write up some notes about the Klinger baby, but couldn't help pausing for a minute with the pen in her hand watching Max.

He was listening intently to the couple and waiting for them to finish, without trying to anticipate their words and interrupt. There was no sign at all that he was impatient or in a hurry or dismissive of their concerns. Now he was writing something down for them and then touching the baby carefully as he explained something else.

There was something about every movement and every expression in his face that inspired confidence, something in his body language that betrayed how much care he had for the babies he was entrusted with.

Or is it only because I love him? she wondered, turning belatedly to Michael Klinger's case notes.

Max startled her a few minutes later by appearing at

the nurses' station himself, still in conversation with one of the N.I.C.U.'s highly trained nurses.

'Thanks for taking so much time with them, Dr Costain,' the older woman was saying. 'They've been driving us a little crazy lately with a lot of questions and a good few accusations, too.'

'They're very nervous about taking Julia home,' he answered, 'now that the time has finally come. And I think they realise that discharge is a long way from being the end of it. I *hope* they realise that! She'll still be on oxygen and a diuretic, and there's still the issue of keeping the right balance between adequate caloric intake and too much fluid. Not to mention the fact that they've got to be super-alert for signs of respiratory illness.'

Paula realised from his words that baby Julia must have bronchopulmonary dysplasia, a serious lung disease caused in part by spending too long on a ventilator after birth when premature lungs were insufficiently developed to function on their own. No wonder the parents had concerns!

The nurse said this herself a moment later, then concluded, 'So you're saying I should cut them more slack today?'

'If you can,' Max answered. 'Although I appreciate that parental anxiety can make them seem like right royal pains. I'm expecting to dread the sound of my pager for Julia's first few weeks after discharge. We just have to try and think, OK, if this were *my* baby…'

His hands formed the vividly realistic shape of someone tenderly cradling a tiny child.

'If this were *my* baby,' he repeated, 'wouldn't I be pestering and yelling and crying and accusing and throwing my weight about if I thought it would help her to get better quicker, help to get her better treatment? Julia's dad is a doctor—a radiologist—and doctors and nurses are always the very worst for that, aren't we?'

He smiled wryly and the N.I.C.U. nurse replied,

'You've got me praying I don't have to discover the hard way that that's true for me. My kids have been textbook perfect so far. But none of them have got to eighteen yet, and I guess even then you don't stop worrying.'

'Worth it, though,' he said seriously. 'It's like a lot of things in life. The hardest things are the most worthwhile.'

'Spoken from experience?'

'Well...I have nieces. Not the same, but it's pretty nice. Kids of my own? Not yet. I hope one day...' He didn't finish, and a moment later the nurse bustled off to the far end of the unit.

Max reached for his tiny patient's file, stepping to the left and brushing Paula's arm with his own, a slow and deliberately sensual gesture. 'Hi...' That was sensual, too, more a caress than a word, but she could barely respond.

If she'd had any doubts after what Janey had said yesterday on the subject of Max wanting children, those doubts could be put aside now. It had been so clear in his tone and in that telling gesture of holding an imaginary baby that the idea of himself as a father was something he'd considered seriously for a long time. It wasn't just something he paid lip service to, or assumed casually that he'd experience at some point—a wife and kids—the automatic adjuncts of a successful man, like a quality car and a beautiful home.

No, Max *wanted* it.

And yet if he marries me...

Marriage hadn't been mentioned, but she was thinking about it, and she was sure he was, too. Little things he'd said a couple of times, such as he was glad he hadn't sold the house when he and Kelly were divorced, although he thought Paula's place was pretty nice, too. Little things, such as had she ever been to France, or Italy, and did she think Europe was too far for a ten-day trip?

Little things. All day they seemed to leap out at her, to ambush her from the deceptive safety of the busy practice routine.

Max, rumpling the shiny dark hair of a three-year-old boy. Max, listening very seriously to the question from a four-year-old girl, 'Are you a doctor at home, too?' and answering carefully, 'Well, I'm always a doctor, but at home I don't usually do doctor *stuff*. I do regular stuff, like eating pizza and watching TV.' Max, talking about basketball to a gangling teenager and about computers to an earnest ten-year-old.

And none of it was an act, she knew. None of it was put on to impress parents or soften kids up. Over dinner tonight they *had* to talk.

Dinner, though, didn't happen. He cancelled at five.

'I've realised it'll be hopeless,' he said. 'I'm on call, and I promised the Beaches that I'd drop round to see baby Julia. Remember, the preemie in the N.I.C.U. this morning? I've got two more patients as well whose parents are probably going to want phone consults. And somehow...' he frowned, then raised his eyebrow quizzically '...I sense that tonight's not the night for us to give ourselves short shrift.'

'No, it's not,' she agreed in a low voice. Don't come out of your office at this precise moment, will you, Deborah? she was thinking. His gaze raked her tightly held face.

'Tomorrow, then?' he said.

'Yes, please.'

Except that by the end of the day she had realised that no amount of talking was going to be enough. No amount was going to be fair to Max. She knew him too well.

'If we talk about it,' she told Kelly Rainer that evening during the six o'clock news, 'he'll say it doesn't matter and we can face it together. But it *does* matter. Stephanie wouldn't give him children, you wouldn't and

I probably can't. I can't ask him to accept that. To tell him I *can't* have kids is a very different thing from telling him I *won't,* though, as you did. He might break off our relationship if I said I didn't want to, but if he knows I want to and *can't*... No, he's too honourable for that. But it would make life hell between us eventually. I've already asked enough of him, having him accept my lost breast.

'So, there's only one thing to do, Kelly. I'll have to break it off.'

And if he heard me now, confiding in the screen image of his former wife, he'd think I was so crazy he'd probably do the breaking off himself! I knew, somehow, that Kelly was going to be important, but I hadn't realised it would be *this.*

'Up next,' Kelly said cheerfully, 'the new Downtown library will open on Saturday. Lots of events not to be missed, especially by families, and all sponsored by Channel Six. Maybe I'll see you there!'

'No, thanks, Kelly, if you don't mind!' Paula said wearily.

CHAPTER NINE

LIFE without Max.

It ought not to have been so hard. After all, they'd only known each other for two months. It hadn't helped, though, that life without Max had got off to a very bad start. To put it mildly, when Paula had tried to tell him there had been something of a scene.

It had happened on Tuesday evening, after he'd had an unusually heavy on call the previous night. He'd been very tired, and had said so as they'd sat down in the same Southwestern restaurant they'd been to for their first meal together that very first day.

She hadn't wanted to come here. Hadn't wanted to eat together at all because she hadn't wanted to make a big deal of it—string it out, put herself in a position where it was difficult to escape—but he had insisted.

'I've *got* to eat, Paula, because I haven't all day, and I really don't feel like just grabbing some junk food. Whatever this is...'

He eyed her. He already knew it was *something.* Knowing that he had recognised her all along for the hopelessly inept liar that she was, Paula had been working herself up to this all day, talking herself into all the myriad reasons why it couldn't and wouldn't have worked anyway, and into a conviction that it actually *wasn't* love—it was just sex, which was classically known for being able to mimic its more lasting counterpart of feeling.

I've been crazy to even *consider* a future to this, she scolded herself more than once. Coming to Arizona, I had it all sewn up—a great life for myself. And if I'd stuck to that, if I hadn't let Max get under my skin…

So it was probably a bad error of judgement, compounding all her other errors of judgement, that she had agreed in the end to eat with him.

And then he announced, 'I'm totally wiped, and in a hell of a mood, I have to say.' He glared around him, as if looking for someone to blame…

'Well, what I'm going to say probably won't improve it,' she told him crisply.

'Yeah?' He barked, then the anger drained from his face and he pressed his palms against his eyes, as if to force away fatigue. 'I'm sorry,' he added. 'Had a run-in with an idiot intern today. I won't take it out on you. Let's start again. You've had a rough day, too?'

He covered her hand with his and began to chafe her knuckles with a gentle caress. 'Don't talk about work. Tell me about pottery or something. Do you want to order straight away or have a drink?' he asked, suddenly achingly warm.

She snatched her hand away. 'You order,' she said. 'I'm not eating. In fact, this won't take long.' She took a deep breath. 'I don't want to prolong this all through dinner so I'll say it now as best I can. Max, I don't want us to see each other any more.' Except that they had to, of course, in the practice. She clarified quickly, 'I don't want us to be personally involved. It was a mistake from the beginning. You've been a wonderful lover. You've restored my body to me in a way I…didn't think was possible…'

Don't cry, Paula, you fool!

'And I'll be grateful to you for that for a long time.'

Good. Much better. Warm, yet guarded. Like the gratitude you'd feel to the doctor who saved your child's life. *Hell, children again!* Sincere and deep but ultimately not fully personal, never crossing over a certain boundary.

'But I'm just not looking for something that's long term. I'm happier alone. And I get the impression you want to have kids. Which I most definitely don't.'

Not can't have, but don't want. Much better. It would convince him that he had rotten luck with women, and that he was perversely attracted to the most *un*maternal types, but that was better for both of them, really. A protection for her, face-saving for him.

She added with a little laugh, 'I just can't imagine that I'd ever enjoy being called Mom!'

Actually, the laugh was rather too tinkly, bearing the same resemblance to her usual laugh that a cheap child's xylophone—*children again*—bore to the full-sized orchestral instrument.

His eyes narrowed ominously and she waited, holding her breath.

'This is crazy!' he bit out, after a moment.

'Oh, really?' She made it as acid as she could.

'Yes! It's coming out of nowhere!'

'Perhaps out of nothing *you've* perceived, but let me tell you—' She broke off.

'OK,' he prompted mercilessly, 'tell me. If you're going to break it off then at least have the decency to be honest about your reasons.'

'Are you suggesting—?'

'I'd like you to do me the courtesy of recognising that I know you pretty well by now, Paula. That's what I'm suggesting. And what you've just said to me is a load of—'

He broke off as an unbearably cheerful waitress bounced up to them. 'Not yet, thanks,' he told her without a glance, and only the last word saved it from being curt to the point of rudeness.

'When you're ready, sir,' the waitress returned, unruffled.

The tiny exchange had given Paula just enough time to marshal her resources. She *had* to do this right because Max had already shown her that he wasn't going to take anything he recognised as dissembling or camouflage.

'If we're going to talk of courtesy,' she attacked the second their waitress was gone, 'then please do *me* the courtesy of not questioning what I say. There's an etiquette to breaking up, Max, and rule number one in the book is that you don't question and you don't argue. If I say that's what I want then it's what I want, OK? And please do not have the unmitigated arrogance to—to— Oh, *hell!*'

Tear-blinded, furious with herself, aching with regret and unable to speak, Paula pushed back her chair and fled. She was no actress...they'd both agreed on that weeks ago...and she ached so desperately to tell him the truth and have him say it didn't matter. She knew he *would* say it, too, but if she let him...if she gave him a chance to be that noble...she was mortally afraid that it would make an imbalance in their relationship that she'd spend the rest of her life trying to correct, and it would poison love for both of them.

'Paula!' He was surging after her, had reached her already and grabbed her arm.

'Let me go!'

'Do you mean that? Do you really mean it because—?'

'I mean it, Max.'

'Then stand by it.' His eyes bored into hers, searching and challenging. 'Because I don't like games. I don't jump through hoops. If there's a problem, air it honestly. And if you're not prepared to do that, you're on your own.'

Exit Paula. End of scene. Very dramatic. Just what she had wanted, going out with an angry bang so that he didn't find out what really was wrong.

At home, half an hour later, all she could think was,

Well, it's over now, as if it had never been, and all that remains for both of us is to put on a good front at work.

Because, of course, life without Max wasn't *really* what the future held. There'd only be life without Max in the personal sense. Professionally...

'I thought you'd want to know that I saw Mickey Walters and his mother this afternoon,' Paula said in her best doctor voice three days later, after knocking on Max's office door just before lunch.

'Yes? Come in.'

'No, this won't take long.' She stood stiffly in the doorway, aware of how silly that was...and how difficult.

'What was he in for?' Max asked, also very professional.

'High fever. Mrs Walters was afraid it was meningitis, but it wasn't. He had no sign of the classic neck pain and stiffness.'

'That's good.'

'What was also good, I thought, was the interaction between Mrs Walters and Mickey. They've been having some counselling, haven't they?'

'Yes. I sent them to Joanne Rivera, who's very good.'

'Well, it's paying off. She was staying much more patient with him, much more involved and attempting to meet him at his own level. As a result, he seemed a lot happier and more confident, even with the listlessness that the fever was producing.'

'Anything from Mrs Walters about his allergies?'

'She hadn't mentioned it so I asked, and she just said that, oh, they'd been much better lately since she'd been following your suggestions about dusting and vacuuming and diet. If things keep going this well, I don't think we'll hear any more about skin tests and injections.'

'I'm pleased to hear it, although it's a pity I couldn't

have seen Mickey myself. But I was squeezed so tight today...'

'You always are,' she pointed out truthfully.

He shrugged. 'I'm one of the senior partners. All our long-time parents recommend us to their friends and the demand just builds. We get Wanda back in a week and a bit. That should ease things somewhat, otherwise we'd have to stop taking on new patients.'

'It's not just that you're one of the senior partners, Max,' Paula said truthfully. 'It's because you're good, and parents recognise the fact. Children, too.'

'Thanks,' he drawled. 'Did I do something special to deserve that? Or were you just throwing out a freebie?'

She flushed and dug her nails into her palms. 'Don't, Max.'

'OK,' he conceded coolly at once. 'I won't. Was that all you wanted to say? About Mickey?'

'Yes. Sorry, I'll...let you finish up.'

Once again she had to recognise her cue to leave, and did so—miserably.

There ought to have been something just a little—if perversely—romantic about this—to have sacrificed her future with Max because of the children he wanted that she couldn't give him. Only somehow it wasn't romantic, not even the slightest bit, because it was just too awkward and painful.

Their scene the other day... She would actually have felt *better,* she concluded now, slumped at the desk in her office, if he had yelled more, fumed, said cruel and utterly unfair things that she could have yelled back at. That icy deliberation of his had been much worse, and everything he'd said had been only too true.

It must have been obvious to everyone on staff that the 'health tonic' Deborah had accused them of taking had got to the end of the bottle. The nursing assistants had been giving Paula sidelong glances and pouring her glasses of iced water before she even asked for them.

Brian kept talking about Wanda's return as if he thought Paula must be feeling horribly overworked.

Well, true, she had arrived very early and stayed very late the past couple of days, but that was to avoid colliding with Max as he came and went.

And Deborah... Deborah started chatting to her about things like fashion and film stars, which was just so far from being the stocky, cheerful pediatrician's normal repertoire of rather blunt, down-to-earth conversation that it was as if her personality had suddenly been taken over by a Talking Barbie.

And then Brian came up with the bright idea of having a partners' lunch at his place the following Sunday to welcome Wanda back.

'Partners and *their* partners, of course,' he added, then clearly wished he hadn't.

It was Friday. The practice had just closed for lunch and the four doctors were gathered in the corridor, about to head their separate ways to eat. Brian looked at Max and Paula, standing as far from each other as decency and space permitted, then looked ostentatiously at his watch and began to sing, very tunelessly, a current and completely maddening advertising jingle.

Deborah said quickly, 'Well, then, Brian, if that's what you want, I guess I can rustle up a date. He'll be gruesome, though.'

'I mean you don't *have* to bring someone,' Brian said, looking quite hunted. Paula felt sorry for her colleague. He couldn't look at his partners, and he'd made an exhaustive study of his watch. What was left? 'Your company solo, Deborah, is always more than pleasant enough to—'

Deborah waved this away. 'Nope. You asked for it, and you'll get it. A date with classic manifestations of level five gruesomeness, and don't say you weren't warned!'

This refreshing return of her non-Talking Barbie persona served to cut the tension, thank goodness, and everyone laughed.

Paula was left dreading the event, though, and nothing that happened in the intervening nine days served to lessen this dread. She saw sick children and well children, she communed with the hummingbirds in her garden, and she went to pottery class, coming home from the latter with several glazed pieces of work that she didn't have a clue what to do with, although in the end one of them received some favourable reviews in its role as a pen-holder on her desk.

With Max, nothing changed, and she missed him more than she would have imagined possible. No phone calls. No desert rambles. No meals together. No nights of lovemaking. And the absolutely last thing she felt like was being with him at a casual social event that centred around a swimming pool. It carried far too many memories of the times they'd spent at his place, soaking away the day's heat in the limpid water.

For much of the event, however, she didn't have to think too much about Max, mainly because, as Deborah had threatened, her date was 'level five gruesome', and he was bad-mannered enough to pursue Paula fairly relentlessly, while seeming to forget Deborah's very existence. The latter, fortunately, found this amusing rather than anything else.

'Where did you get him, Deb?' Paula sang ominously out of the side of her mouth when Vaughan went off in search of his fifth beer.

'The mountain bikers I ride with sometimes,' she said. 'He kind of did the knight-in-shining-armour thing for me one day when I had a bad fall that no one else saw. Brushed me off, put me and my bike in his van and took us out to dinner.'

'Us?'

'Well, me, I guess. The bike stayed in the van. So anyway, I owed him a favour, and since I was forced to politely decline the favour that was *his* first choice…' her drawl made it quite clear what sort of a favour she meant '…I proposed this as a substitute.'

'You're only encouraging him, you know,' Paula pointed out.

'I know. As little as possible, though, believe me. Do you think I'm bad? I *do* owe him, but I just can't respond to a man who tells me he's heard women doctors are hot lovers because they know all the good nerve endings, and would I please demonstrate them so as to improve his technique! So thanks for drawing his fire, Paula!'

'Oh, my pleasure,' she drawled back.

'It's certainly making Max jealous,' Deborah pointed out bluntly.

Paula's head flew up instinctively and she flushed. She didn't want to know about Max's emotional state. It was too hard! She had avoided looking at him, avoided being anywhere near him, whenever possible.

That hadn't been difficult. As well as the charming Vaughan, there was Brian's wife, Linda, to chat to, and Wanda's new baby to admire. Little Nicholas had his mother's Polish features and colouring—big, fair, round-faced and adorable. Wanda's husband Jim was nice, too, and their other two children, aged six and three, were earnestly and unselfconsciously cute.

Brian's kids were older and a little standoffish, no longer willing to entrust their most important thoughts to strangers as Wanda's Alexander and Elizabeth were, but they added to the gathering and provided convenient bodies at times for Paula to strategically position herself on the opposite side of. She really hadn't allowed Vaughan Blackett all that much of her time.

Yet Max had noticed, and minded about it.

What are we doing to each other? How much of it can we take? Will it go away? Or will I end up leaving the practice because it's just too hard?

Tortured by all this, Paula couldn't manage a response

to Deborah's blunt observation and got herself away to a place where she could think—over at the table in the shade of the house where salads, drinks and other accompaniments to the meal were laid out.

Pouring herself a long glass of mineral water and juice, she dared to look across at Max. He was in the pool, his arms stretched along the lip that ran around it level with the blue water line, and his torso and legs floating horizontally, buoying themselves up every now and then with a flurry of lazy kicking. He didn't look very comfortable, and he didn't look very happy.

He *did* look thoughtful, lost in it to the point where she wondered if he'd even hear someone addressing him.

What have we done to each other? she thought miserably again. Who'd have thought it could possibly get to the point of causing this much pain and confusion in so short a time? Why didn't I think ahead? Why didn't I realise that fertility was the issue, far more than the way my body looks? I should have been stronger at the beginning, and never let anything happen at all!

Except that this would have been impossible. And not to have known his love-making... *That* idea was so arid and frightening that it was unthinkable.

She saw Vaughan begin to wander purposefully in her direction and thought, No! Not now. I don't want *anyone* right now!

She went towards the house, then at the last minute, with her hand already poised on the sliding patio door, something made her pause and turn, and there was Max's gaze, sizzling across the space that separated them and bathing her instantly with heat and awareness.

She fled inside. The neat, spacious, modern house was silent. Everyone was out by the pool. There was a bathroom on this level, but she craved greater privacy so she padded barefoot up the stairs, still wearing only her swimsuit, until she came to the open door of Brian's and Linda's bedroom, off which opened a large, luxurious master bathroom—skylighted, mirrored and equipped with a hot tub of decadent dimensions.

Its chrome taps gleamed and Paula smiled a little. She had heard Brian confess that it was almost never used. These days, who had the time?

It had seats of a sort around it, though, padded vinyl cushions, so Paula chose one and sat down with her feet on the tiled surrounds of the huge tub, hugging her slim knees and resting her chin there.

I won't leave the practice, she decided at once. Whatever happens, I won't run away. Not when I've wanted to make this change for so long. I ought to be able to at least *envisage* the possibility that this will get better, but somehow I can't. Why?

The question was destined to remain unanswered just then.

She heard a movement in the doorway of the bedroom and looked up, half expecting it to be Vaughan, leeringly pleased at having successfully pursued her into solitude, but it wasn't Vaughan at all.

It was Max.

His body was freshly towelled, his white swimming trunks clung and his feet were bare. She straightened warily and pivoted to stretch her legs down to the floor, ready to stand. To escape, if she could. But he closed the bedroom door behind him, entered the bathroom and closed its door as well, underlining the fact that they were *very* alone.

'Hi,' she said inadequately. The word had a hollow sound, as speech did in a tiled bathroom. The diffuse sunlight shafted, blurred by the opaque white plastic of the skylight, onto his face and shoulders.

'Paula,' he said, his voice both husky and commanding, 'we can't let this go. I've seen how horrible these two weeks have been for you. It's been as bad for me. Worse… I was wrong in what I said at the restaurant. I *won't* let this go! We have to confront it!'

'Confront—?' The word caught in her throat.

She didn't know what he meant, didn't even suspect as he came towards her.

Then suddenly she was in his arms, trembling with need and release, pulled apart by the feel of his cool skin against her and his hot mouth roving over her face, her neck, her shoulders. It was so intensely *right* to be with him, to be touching him again, that she couldn't question it yet, just had to close her eyes and *feel.* It wasn't until he began to peel the thin straps of her suit from her shoulders, down over her arms, that she knew the first moment of panic.

What was he doing? How could she find the strength to resist *this?*

'I can't let you call the tune on this, Paula.' His voice was low and vibrant with feeling. 'There are some occasions when a man has to be masterful, and this is one of them! You've never let me see you without clothes. All those glorious times when we made love, and it was always in darkness.

'I didn't even realise it until I thought back—hell, I've been doing nothing *but* think back on what we had together—and that was all I could come up with. Nothing else made sense. That you were still so scared of how your body looked that you ran from me rather than face it. But look at yourself in this big, bright mirror, Paula! God, woman, you're *beautiful!*'

She looked, felt herself trembling, felt the tightening of her throat. He'd got it wrong... Yes, she'd masked their love-making in darkness and dressed when his back was safely turned. It was a hurdle, and one she knew she'd been on the point of clearing on the day of Janey's barbecue. But it wasn't the real problem.

That he could think it was, though. That he'd clearly been questing so hard for understanding after his first angry reaction. That he was prepared to go this far for her...

He stood behind her now, with his left arm wrapped around her shoulder and down across her waist, while his right hand pulled the still just damp swimsuit slowly lower and lower—past her armpits, her breast, her waist, her hips—until finally it dropped the length of her slim legs to the floor.

The way he was holding her, his left forearm would have lifted and nudged the underside of her breast if she'd still had a breast on that side. As it was, the fine hairs of his arm brushed only the smooth skin beneath her pale, healed scar.

'Look,' he said softly. 'I can see your heart beating. I've felt it before when we've made love. Now I can see it.'

She saw it, too, and watched it for a long moment, wonderingly. The visible pulse of it hopped between her ribs, the size of one of the hummingbirds in her garden.

'You're *alive,* Paula,' he told her urgently. 'And you have just one small flaw that prevents you from being totally whole, while the rest of you—' His breath caught in his throat. 'Your legs, this flat, delicious, vanilla pudding of a stomach, this wonderful sensitive breast here, so high and neat, these tantalising shoulders and, yes, even the scar. See, I'm touching it now, and you're watching me do it. I love you more every day, and I've felt us both blossoming as that grows between us.'

He bent to sear his lips against the curve of her neck and shoulder. 'Please trust me. Please trust your body. I love it and you so much...'

She shuddered and a convulsive sob broke from her. To hear him say all this, words of commitment and caring that she never thought she'd hear from a man again, to know and feel how much he meant every word of it, to realise how much it was healing all that had still been scarred and sealed off in her soul when she'd come to Arizona...

And to know that he'd got it all wrong. The issue of

her nakedness was there, but it was manageable. He'd just proved that to her as they'd both watched his caresses in the mirror. But the issue of children…

She hadn't had a period since she'd arrived in Arizona, and that was well over two months ago now. Not that it was anything unusual, either. On the contrary, it was par for the course. She often went three or four months without one. More! After the end of her chemo five years ago, she hadn't bled through an entire Ohio winter and spring.

Max's arms were still around her, still caressing, and his mouth still moved on her skin as he watched her face intently in the mirror. She sobbed again, and her wavering resolve firmed again.

He didn't deserve this! He deserved better!

'No, Max!' she managed. 'No!'

She fled, grabbing her suit off the floor and a towel from the rail to shield herself, running naked to hide in one of the children's bedrooms while she put it on and not pausing, for the first time in five years, to check that everything was sitting right.

Down at the poolside a minute later, she found that everyone was now absorbed in helping themselves to plates of food as they chatted animatedly. It was easy enough to grab her sundress and put it on, pick up her bag and towel and gabble to Brian and Linda, 'I'm not feeling well, I'm sorry. I won't stay to eat. I'd better get home.'

She missed Deborah's concerned movement towards her, but then catapulted full into Vaughan Blackett, who seized the opportunity and drawled creamily with what was evidently intended as humour, 'I knew you found me irresistible, sweetheart, but there's no need to be so eager about it.'

Of course she could not simply fight him off with violence as instinct clamoured she should. 'I'm sorry, Vaughan, I—'

'Don't apologise, Paula, please! Now, calm down and catch your breath.'

'I have to go.'

'Not without giving me your phone number…'

'I really am sorry, I must—'

'And, anyway, I was just coming to ask someone, since you're all doctors. Is that little girl all right face down in the pool like that?'

'What?' Her glance flew to the water and there was Wanda's three-year-old Elizabeth, ominously motionless with her hair floating around her head like pale seaweed and her limbs shimmering in the light. *'How long…?'*

She didn't wait for an answer, and at that moment Wanda herself let out a scream. *'Elizabeth!'*

But someone else was quicker.

Max. He must have seen the child from an upstairs window. He had catapulted from the house, sprinted to the pool and dived flat out across the water before Paula had covered half the distance.

Behind her, she heard Brian saying urgently, 'Give me the baby, Wanda. Don't try to run. Max is there! Hold her, Deborah, she can hardly stand.'

Wanda's husband, Jim, groaned and stammered brokenly, 'I just checked on her a minute ago! God! Was it only a minute ago? Please, God, it was only a minute ago. I told her not to go in the water. I told her…' His words trailed off into sounds of anguish as he stumbled towards the pool.

Max had the little girl now, and Paula herself reached the poolside just ahead of Jim as Max gathered Elizabeth in his arms and strode chest deep through the water to lift her to the hot, tiled surround. Vaughan was saying to no one in particular, 'I *thought* she looked a bit little, but she seemed so confident… It was only a minute, and then I started to wonder if something was wrong.'

'We were both watching her,' Jim was saying, 'both

checking on her. But we got caught up in the baby and—Oh, God, it can happen so fast!'

Max and Paula wasted no time in starting to work over the little girl. He was already beside her shoulders, positioning her correctly to begin mouth-to-mouth resuscitation while Paula reached for her wrist in search of a pulse. She found one almost at once and felt its strength and rhythm with a rush of intense physical relief.

'Yes! Yes!' She almost shouted it. 'Strong and steady!'

'But she's not breathing,' Max murmured, so low that no one else could have heard, and then began his task, completely focused, while Paula felt her skin crawl with dread. Thank God it's Max! was the only rational thought that crystallised in her mind. And thank God he saw it from upstairs because even those few seconds it would have taken Jim or me to reach her…

It seemed like an eternity and nothing was happening. She could almost feel the force of Max's will and determination, like heat from a fire radiating to her skin. Wanda was beside them now, every movement and every sound she made betraying her helpless anguish. 'Elizabeth! Elizabeth! It's Mommy, darling. Come on! Come on, Elizabeth!'

And Max had been in time. Suddenly water gushed and spluttered from the child's lungs. She gave a sobbing, choking gasp as Max quickly lifted her, then she writhed to double over in his arms and vomit pool water all over his thighs.

'Oh, thank God!' Everyone said it, but it was Max's voice that Paula was echoing under her breath.

Elizabeth reached for her mother and Wanda held her as if they were glued together. The little girl was still coughing and struggling, and Wanda herself was trembling like the leaves of an aspen tree, though she summoned a soothing, cheerful tone as she said to the pale, crying child, 'Goodness, that wasn't much fun, was it?

But you're all right now. You're fine now. Next time we'll just put our feet in, won't we? Just go in with Mommy next time, won't you, sweetheart?'

Paula stayed only long enough to satisfy herself that Elizabeth really was quite all right, steeled all the while against the possibility of Max confronting her again. He was still too caught up in what had happened, though, calming the Hunts down and carefully deflecting any hostility from Vaughan, who continued to mouth complacently that he had *wondered* if something might be wrong.

There was just one moment when Max's control broke.

'Next time,' he said ominously to the other man, 'don't wonder, OK? Act!'

Paula took this as her own cue to pick up her things and slip away under the safe cover of the buzz of concern that still filled the air. Elizabeth was fine, and there was nothing more she could do. If Max had tried to follow her, she didn't stay long enough to find out.

It was only at home, late that night, as she undressed for bed and relived his touch on her skin in the accidental brush of her own fingers, that she became aware for the first time of the new lump that seemed to have appeared out of nowhere in her right breast.

CHAPTER TEN

PANIC attacks. Cancer survivors were prone to them.

'I have cancer all the time!' Paula's good friend and fellow breast cancer survivor, Diane, in Ohio, had confessed to her once. 'Rampaging, rip-roaring, runaway cancer of every possible kind. Sometimes it takes a week to claim my life. Sometimes it takes ten years to run its course. If I scratch a mole it's skin cancer. If I feel extra tired it's leukaemia. If I cough it's lung cancer from breathing the smoke of other people's cigarettes. And heaven help me if I ever have a pain!'

Paula had laughed at the time. She had the same repertoire of doom-laden scenarios that would ambush her out of the blue, usually as the time for her next check-up drew near. When her oncologist in Ohio had told her she could extend the time between check-ups to a year, she had begged him to keep it at six months, knowing that as each month went by she got more nervous.

She *still* had them every six months. She was due for her first one in Arizona soon—in six weeks, actually—and had already spoken by phone with the cancer specialist who had been recommended to her by her Ohio doctor, and praised also by Brian.

There was no way she was going to wait six weeks now, though. Trying to make herself stay calm, she lay on her back on the rug in her living-room, placed her right arm up behind her head and felt her breast carefully with her left hand. She used the pads of her three middle fingers and began at the edge of her nipple, moving out to the rim of the breast and up her chest towards her armpit.

The whole breast felt lumpy and sore, swollen, *different.*

Diane says she doesn't panic about that any more because it always happens before her period, but I've never had that... There's the old saying that if it hurts it isn't cancer, but I know that's not always true... It's come so suddenly, but it *can* come suddenly—just a few weeks, sometimes, can make all the difference.'

No matter how she tried to rationalise it, the fear wouldn't go away. No matter how much she told herself that panic was pointless, and she should just resolve to call her doctor first thing in the morning and put the whole thing out of her mind until she knew more, it buzzed there all night long, it seemed, like a swarm of angry bees, and she barely slept.

She called her new oncologist's appointment line from the phone in her office at eight-thirty the next morning and was put on hold for several minutes, thus delaying the start of her own patient list for the day. She never caught up, knew she was more distracted than she should be and was thankful that everything was routine.

Encountering Wanda several times at the coffee-station or along the corridor, she knew that the latter would get the impression on her first day back after her maternity leave that Dr Nichols was disorganised and perpetually harried. She enquired about Elizabeth's well-being and was, of course, pleased to hear that the little girl had eaten like a horse at dinner-time and had slept like an angel all night, but even this news couldn't make her forget the new foreboding that shadowed every thought.

And encountering Max...

To have had him for support during this crisis—phantom or real—would have been heart-achingly wonderful. Yet the selfless part of her, the part of her that loved him so much it felt like a potent drug, was thankful that this didn't have to be *his* ordeal, too.

They had maintained a polite façade this morning, after her emotional departure from Brian's yesterday, but beneath the façade she was convinced that he wasn't ready to let the issue rest. If it hadn't been for little Elizabeth's drama yesterday, he would have followed her. He had probably been trying to gauge her intentions and her state by looking down from the window upstairs and that was how he had happened to see the ominous sight in the pool.

I have to tell him, she thought. About the issue of my fertility. And about this new lump. We both care too much. Yesterday proved that. These secrets are just too huge... But *after* my appointment, when I have more concrete knowledge about what's going on.

The appointment was fixed for the next day at eleven, which meant she had to ask Susan, who scheduled the practice's workload, to arrange cover for her. It was tight. She would be away for a good two hours altogether, although some of it would be during lunch and fortunately Dr Pressman's office suite was only ten minutes' drive away in the direction of downtown. In the end the load was spread between Wanda, Max and Deborah, as Brian was off tomorrow, too.

'What, urgent emergency shopping spree?' Deborah asked when she found out about it.

'No, doctor's appointment,' Paula returned, ready to begin the process of becoming a little more open about her history now.

Holding it all back had lately started to make it all into a bigger issue than she was now happy with five and a half years down the track. It was probably time she told the other practice partners about her cancer, especially if this new lumpiness—

Too late, she realised that Max had appeared from his office in time to hear her words to Deborah, and his eyes were boring into her, shocked.

How can he *read* me the way he does? she wondered frantically.

'Not feeling well, Paula?' he murmured to her as soon as Deborah had gone, and there was much more than just casual enquiry behind the words.

'Just my annual pap,' she improvised, and, as always, he knew she was lying.

'Damn it, Paula,' he rasped. 'Why are you making this so *impossible?* Why won't you let me—?' He broke off sharply as nursing assistant Vicky Domingo came past, bearing several charts.

There wasn't time to pursue any of this now, of course, and Paula managed to avoid him for the rest of the day. When the phone rang several times that night she let the machine pick up and listened, suppressing tears, to the tender, then frustrated, then urgent messages he left.

He even came round, and she actually hid in the spare bedroom and watched him through a slit in the curtains as he paced outside her front door, before conceding defeat and driving away. Her car was safely hidden in the garage. He couldn't *know* that she was home. He wouldn't challenge her about it tomorrow morning, would he?

After he'd gone, she called her parents in Florida, Chris in New York and Diane in Ohio to tell each of them about her new fear. Each time she began by making fun of herself, then cried, then made fun of herself again. Chris gave her sympathy, her parents gave her love but Diane was the only one who totally understood. But even she was still very safely and happily married to the man she'd loved since college, and had had no recurrence of her disease now in seven years.

Paula ended the evening feeling very down, and almost, *almost* called Max. No... No! Not until I have some hard facts. It wouldn't help either of us to thrash the whole thing through now.

And she did *not* watch the Channel Six news.

'I want a mammogram, a blood test and a bone scan,' Paula said to Dr Thomas Pressman, knowing that this assertiveness was a symptom of her panic but unable to do anything about it.

'Well, let's start with a manual breast exam and, yes, a blood test, and decide where to go from there,' he answered soothingly.

Soothingly? Paula hated that!

She resisted the temptation to stress her own professional status and simply *demand* a bone scan. Resisted because *he* already knew she was a doctor, and *she* already knew she was being unreasonable. But she wondered just why Dr Mencken in Ohio had been so convinced she would like this man!

'Hmm,' he was saying.

Hmm? What sort of a diagnosis is that?

She was lying on his examination table, naked from the waist up and covered with a paper sheet. A doctor getting a nasty taste of her own medicine, as Dr Pressman palpated her right breast carefully, an action he must have performed on literally thousands of women.

'Hmm,' he said again, after a minute. 'There is definitely something, isn't there? I have to say, though, it doesn't feel like cancer.'

A flood of sweet relief? No! Because she didn't believe him!

'I assure you, though, Dr Pressman, my breast doesn't usually feel like this, and I still want—'

'A bone scan. I know. It doesn't, though, huh?'

'Huh'? That was even worse than 'hmm'! Now he was frowning down at the long questionnaire about her history that she and his nurse had compiled together, then he flipped it aside to study the photocopied notes from her case file in Ohio, sent by Dr Mencken.

'Now, you do say it's tender?' he probed now.

'A little, yes.'

'And there is…uh…nothing obvious that you can think of, yeah?'

'Uh' and 'yeah' now. This man's repertoire of expressive sounds was huge!

'No. There isn't. So if I could schedule a—'

'OK, yes…' Just waving her words aside completely! 'We'll have the nurse take blood, we'll schedule a fine needle biopsy and if you can give her a urine sample as well,' he finished.

'A urine sample?'

'Covering the bases,' he replied enigmatically, while she was flipping through a mental Merck *Manual of Diagnosis and Therapy* in her mind.

He expected to find exactly *what* in her urine?

'Evidence of bladder or kidney tumour, *obviously!*' said the area of her brain where all her really *splendid* panic attacks came from.

'OK,' she replied weakly. 'Will you…will you have a result on that straight away?'

'Pretty much,' he answered, with a horrible degree of good cheer.

Loathing him, Paula lay beneath her sheet until he'd left the room, then dressed again and went out to produce her specimen, apologising to the nurse a minute later. 'Sorry, I've sweated all over the cup.'

The nurse, Pat—about Paula's own age, pleasant, and very married-looking—smiled sympathetically, then disappeared.

'Sorry, Dr Pressman, what was it that you wanted this tested for?' Paula heard her say along the corridor. Dr Pressman's reply wasn't audible.

The test must have been pretty good because it didn't take long. But perhaps that meant it was *bad,* unreliable, outdated…

I'm going to *insist* on that bone scan! Paula was thinking, as Pat called her in from the waiting room again with a smile.

'Does...does your expression...uh...mean that it's good news?' Paula managed.

'Well, if it was me, I'd think so,' Pat said chirpily and left her at the mercy of Dr Pressman in his private office.

He dropped the bomb a minute later. 'I guess you didn't realise you were pregnant, huh?'

Pregnant?

The room went yellow, then purple, then black, all in lovely pretty patterns.

'Max...' she breathed, then, with fuzzy wonder, *'Max...!'*

Dr Pressman caught her just in time.

He was hovering over her, looking rather concerned, when the room righted itself and resumed its proper colour scheme some minutes later. She was vaguely aware that he and Nurse Pat had been whispering urgent words to each other and that they'd asked her a question or two, but she'd been too dizzy and faint to reply.

'I guess you *really* didn't realise you were pregnant!' Dr Pressman said.

He had settled her back into the easy chair she had tried to rise from after his stunning announcement, and now Pat appeared with water and a concerned expression.

'You poor thing,' she said. 'I called your office and told them you were delayed here. The testing strip didn't go all that dark so I'd say you're not that far along, but obviously you're far enough for your body to be doing weird things.'

'It was the shock,' Paula said, only able to be simply honest. 'I thought I was sterile after the chemo I had five years ago. I thought I had a recurrence in my right breast.'

'Don't try to talk yet,' Dr Pressman said. 'Pat, can you get her something to eat? You look tired, Dr

Nichols. I imagine with this scare you haven't been eating or sleeping properly…'

'No,' she admitted. 'And I'm sorry about all those demands. I guess the bone scan can wait for now.'

'We'll still take the blood test to set your mind at rest,' he promised, 'but I'd say all we'll find that's unusual is elevated pregnancy hormone levels. I'm not sure if you want to consider the implications of pregnancy in relation to cancer—'

'I don't,' she answered, without even letting him finish.

'Yes, basically, I'd support that decision, in your case. Then that means…?'

'I want this baby very much.'

'In that case, Dr Nichols, congratulations. I'll look forward to conferring with your obstetrician, and I'm happy to recommend someone if you'd like.'

Paula laughed and waved her arms. 'I—'

'Too much to deal with right now?'

'Just a bit.' She laughed again.

'Then… Look, I do have another patient waiting now…'

'Get to her, then,' Paula nodded. 'I know how it is.'

Pat returned with a packet of corn chips, a doughnut, and an apologetic expression. 'Not exactly a nutritious prenatal snack, sorry.'

'That's OK.' She heard the continuing weakness in her own voice. This still seemed so unreal…

And five minutes later, when Max appeared…

She gazed in disbelief as he almost exploded into the room in Pat's wake. His face was white beneath his tan and his temples and hairline were damp, and when he took off those silver-lensed glasses his eyes burned.

'Paula!' It was nothing like his normal voice.

She tried to rise, her knees weak all over again, and he pulled her against him, his hands claw-like in their grip. Pat murmured something and disappeared.

'Melissa told me there'd been a message from Pressman's office that you'd fainted and would be late back. God, you have to tell me, darling, what did he say? What did they find?'

No words would come, just tears. Floods of them, making speech impossible although she struggled to tell him. She didn't have a clue why she was reacting like this. What was there to cry about? Just *him,* of course, and the fact that he was here, and holding her.

'I'm— I'm—' She choked, her whole body convulsed and she just couldn't say it. The breath control wasn't there.

'Shh… Shh…' he soothed. 'Whatever it is, we'll get through it together, OK? Is *this* what Tuesday two weeks ago was about? And Sunday? Don't *ever* do this to me…to *us*…again, Paula! Don't keep it from me! Even in the last five years there have been huge advances in the way they treat breast cancer, especially when you're vigilant about check-ups and self-examination and catch it early.

'And if it's spread too far…we'll get married as soon as we can, and just live out the time we have. Only we'll do it *together,* Paula, because I want you. I love you, for God's sake, and I'm just not putting up a second longer with what you've been dishing me lately! OK?'

'O-OK…' Control was returning at last, though she still possessed no capacity to be subtle at the moment. 'Max, I'm—pregnant.'

'What?'

'You're right.' Her body still jerked with ebbing sobs, but she could speak now. 'I thought it was cancer, and until about twenty minutes ago I also thought I was probably sterile. The sterility was why… Max, I know how much you want children. Janey told me. And I know how you've been disappointed twice before, with Stephanie and Kelly. I couldn't have done that to you again. That's why I tried to end it, to stop seeing you. But now...'

'We're having a baby...' he breathed, a smile dawning in his face. 'Can't believe it! *Really* can't believe it! How? *When?*'

'Two weeks ago, when you'd run out of protection and I told you it didn't matter. I really thought it didn't. I hadn't menstruated since coming to Arizona. But I guess my body does produce eggs every now and then, and this time...'

'This time, we hit the jackpot,' he whispered, and their lips met.

It was a clumsy kiss, but that didn't matter. Paula's lips were still trembling and Max was still breathing hard. Also, they were both laughing.

Or crying, maybe? Paula honestly didn't know, and she doubted whether Max did either. Perhaps crying and laughing were the same thing sometimes, she decided hazily, stirred to the depths of her being. To go from contemplating death to anticipating new life in a matter of moments... To realise, as she now took in all he had said, that Max had declared his love and need for her even when he'd thought their life together might be measured in months...

She wound her arms more tightly around him, thinking, How has this happened? How have I deserved this happiness?

And then all thought was swept away in the strength of her response to him. Their kiss wasn't clumsy any more, but wild and deep and spreading. His hands were in her hair, his lips at her throat, his words tangled and fervent and totally incomprehensible in her ear. Was he just saying her name?

'Max, oh, Max,' she whispered in return.

Fortunately Dr Pressman—wonderful Dr Pressman, who could say 'uh' and 'yeah' and 'hmm' as much as he liked from now on—didn't seem to be using his office much this morning. In fact, the place was fairly quiet, and Max broke off long enough to say teasingly, 'How convenient that your appointment was just before lunch!'

'I guess we don't have for ever, though,' she frowned, thinking of this afternoon's appointments.

'As far as I'm concerned, that's exactly what we *do* have,' he countered seriously. 'For ever. The rest of our lives.'

'Max, this disease can recur.'

'Shh...'

'And there are some oncologists who'd say it would increase my risk to carry this baby to term.'

'I don't care what some oncologists say,' he responded quietly. 'What do *you* say, Paula? Do you have any fear that a pregnancy would jeopardise your health? Do you *want* this baby? I'll support you in whatever you decide.'

'Do I want this baby?' she said, then answered soberly, 'More than anything I've ever wanted in my life.' Meaning every word. 'I don't care about fears. Yes, I'll probably have a few. Panic attacks, like I've had for the past couple of days. Phantom lumps in my breast. A horrible dread of every test result. I...may be a bit hard to live with sometimes. But no one is guaranteed a long life and, realistically, I know the risk is very small now. As long as you're there with me...'

He laughed. 'Listen, a few minutes ago I thought I was going to be there with you while you went through cancer surgery and chemo and your hair fell out and you were nauseous for weeks on end.'

'We might still get that last part,' she pointed out.

'I'll lay in a supply of crisp, crunchy crackers and nice, salty potato chips immediately,' he teased. 'But do you know what I'm saying, Paula? It's in the marriage vows, you know.' Now his voice was probing and serious, and she responded in the same way.

'Yes, and I can't wait for the day when I'll say it to

you—"For better for worse, in sickness and in health." In front of everyone we love. Because I'll mean it from the bottom of my heart, Max,' she promised him.

'I think we both already do…' he answered, and bent once again to find her mouth with his.

Outside, with an indulgent smile on her face, Nurse Pat quietly taped a quickly written notice to the office door. Just as on the door of a hotel honeymoon suite, it read, DO NOT DISTURB.

...there's more to the story!

Superromance.
A *big* satisfying read about unforgettable characters. Each month we offer *six* very different stories that range from family drama to adventure and mystery, from highly emotional stories to romantic comedies—and much more! Stories about people you'll believe in and care about. Stories too compelling to put down....

Our authors are among today's *best* romance writers. You'll find familiar names and talented newcomers. Many of them are award winners—and you'll see why!

If you want the biggest and best in romance fiction, you'll get it from Superromance!

Emotional, Exciting, Unexpected...

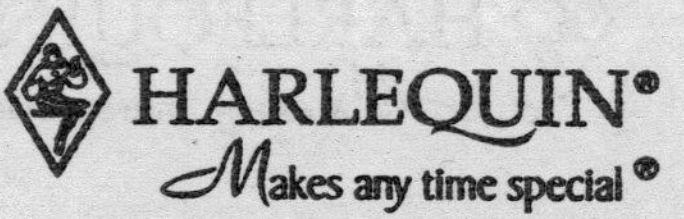

Visit us at www.eHarlequin.com

HSDIR1